11/16

IT'S NOT ME, IT'S YOU

IT'S
NOT ME,
IT'S

YOU

stephanie kate strohm

Point

Library of Congress Cataloging-in-Publication Data available

ISBN 978-0-545-95258-3

10 9 8 7 6 5 4 3 2 1   16 17 18 19 20

Printed in the U.S.A.   23

First edition, November 2016
Book design by Ellen Duda

IT'S NOT ME, IT'S YOU

stephanie kate strohm

Point

All rights reserved. Published by Point, an imprint of Scholastic Inc., *Publishers since 1920.* SCHOLASTIC, POINT, and associated logos are trademarks and/or registered trademarks of Scholastic Inc.

The publisher does not have any control over and does not assume any responsibility for author or third-party websites or their content.

Library of Congress Cataloging-in-Publication Data available

ISBN 978-0-545-95258-3

10 9 8 7 6 5 4 3 2 1   16 17 18 19 20

Printed in the U.S.A.   23

First edition, November 2016
Book design by Ellen Duda

For the Strohmberries. Today, I've got a story.

A MERE SEVENTEEN YEARS AGO, A BEAUTIFUL blond baby was born in sunny San Anselmo, California. That baby was named Avery Dennis, and over the next seventeen years, she proceeded to date more hotties than most people date in a lifetime, to run the Prom Committee like it was her job, and to pretty much crush it, generally speaking. However, an unfortunate incident in the spring of her senior year changed everything, sending the formerly formidable Avery Dennis tumbling into a pit of doubt and despair.

This is the story of how Avery Dennis overcame adversity, decided she was done with dating, and against all the odds, changed the landscape of San Anselmo Prep's senior prom forever.

Now that the legendary prom night of Avery Dennis has come to a close, the girls and boys—*especially the boys*—who bore witness to this historic event have come together to discuss the long and winding path that led Avery Dennis to her moment of greatness. Here, for the first time ever, is the complete and authoritative oral history of Avery Dennis's dating life. I present to you, Ms. Segerson, "It's Not Me, It's You: An Oral History of Boys."
    —*Avery Dennis*

Avery, you clearly misunderstood the assignment. Please see me after class.
    —*Ms. Segerson*

THE BEGINNING

AVERY DENNIS, *me*: I had an epiphany in the place one is least likely to have an epiphany: American history class.

MS. SEGERSON, *surprisingly stylish history teacher*: To be honest, Avery is not always completely engaged in class. She takes copious notes, but they seem to be more of an excuse to use an entire rainbow spectrum of pens than to actually record the lecture. But there was something different about the day we first discussed oral history.

AVERY: Oral history is basically talking. It's like when you interview people about events they witnessed, and then you learn about the events from lots of different perspectives. See? I do take copious notes.

MS. SEGERSON: The assignment was to interview several adults about an event in American history that they had lived through.

AVERY: But the assignment was the least important thing. Especially because we're seniors. It's spring semester. Like, who cares?

MS. SEGERSON: Oh, I cared *very* much about the assignment. And Avery's final GPA cared about the assignment. And I bet the Admissions Committee at Pepperdine would care, too, if I happened to give them a call.

AVERY: I cared *very* much about the assignment. Especially when Ms. Segerson said that oral histories could help us understand *why* certain events had happened. And that there's no time limit on history. Like, even if something just happened, it can still be history. Especially if what had just happened was an event of such horrible and epic proportions, it could barely be spoken of aloud.

MS. SEGERSON: At least Avery was keeping things in perspective. Imagine if she'd overreacted.

Editor's Note: Ms. Segerson hadn't been this sarcastic in September.—AD

AVERY: I had aged years in only a matter of days, and it was all because of . . . the incident.

THE INCIDENT

NATALIE WAGNER, *random freshman:* Avery Dennis was the closest thing to a legend the senior class had.

BECCA HORN, *random freshman:* Avery Dennis was a known clone. It was like she'd watched a bunch of '90s high school sitcoms and invented herself. The world did not need a third Wakefield twin.

> *Editor's Note: The Wakefields are fictional California teens from a book series. Although this remark was clearly intended as a burn, they seemed pretty awesome when I googled them. Also, I was starting to understand what Ms. Segerson meant about history being subjective. And the perils of unreliable sources.*

NATALIE, *random but very wise freshman:* Like, I'm not saying that if Avery Dennis wore army pants and flip-flops, *I'd* wear army pants and flip-flops, but everybody knows who Avery Dennis is.

BECCA, *random and very disgruntled freshman:* Yeah, I know who Avery Dennis is. Everybody knows who everybody is because this stupid school only has like sixty kids in each grade.

NATALIE: Avery Dennis was definitely popular. And, like, why is anybody popular, you know? Is that really something you can even define? Like, what *is* popularity? Why are popular people popular? Popularity is just like this ineffable thing. You're either popular or you're not. And Avery Dennis definitely was.

BECCA: Sure, I guess you could say Avery Dennis had it. If by *it*, you mean a lobotomy.
 Editor's Note: Unreliable sources.

NATALIE: She and her friends ate lunch every day in the best spot outside. She went to, like, every party that was actually a good party. She'd broken some kind of state tennis record. Her hair was like a golden veil.

BECCA: There is absolutely nothing remarkable whatsoever about Avery Dennis.

NATALIE: But perhaps most crucially of all, Avery Dennis had never been single. Ever. And I don't mean just in this year that I'd been in school with her. Everybody knows that Avery Dennis has always had a boyfriend. Even when she was, like, in utero.

BECCA: Truly boring people are terrified of being alone. That tells you everything you need to know about the dating history of Avery Dennis.

NATALIE: She'd dated all the hottest guys at San Anselmo Prep. And most of the hottest guys at Sir Francis Drake High. And a certain TV star. And even, if you believe the rumors, a minor-league soccer player and the heir to the throne of a small European principality.

Editor's Note: Sometimes rumors are just rumors.

NATALIE: It was almost surprising that she *hadn't* dated Luke Murphy before senior year, you know? They just went together perfectly. Avery Dennis couldn't have even built herself a better boyfriend in a lab! I mean, if there was a lab where you could, like, build boyfriends. Once they finally got together, you would see them walking down the halls and be like, yes, that is the golden couple.

BECCA: No, I wouldn't have called Luke Murphy and Avery Dennis the golden couple. Firstly, that's not a phrase I would use. Ever. And secondly, two people aren't a golden couple just because they're both blonds. Also, two blond people shouldn't date. It looks weird, like they're going to start singing "Tomorrow Belongs to Me."

NATALIE: I think it was all part of a master plan. Like, she didn't want to date Luke Murphy too soon, because she had known since kindergarten that he would be the *perfect* senior prom date. Some people just have heads that were built to wear a crown. Luke Murphy has a prom king head. Maybe it's his jawline?

: I didn't even know that Luke Murphy and Avery Dennis were dating until after she went crazy. Because I have my own life. I cannot be bothered to keep up with the unending carousel that is Avery Dennis's Boyfriend of the Month.

NATALIE: They had their differences, though. Luke was the captain of the lacrosse team and the Student Council president. Avery was the captain of the tennis team and head of the Prom Committee. Very different.

BECCA: Luke Murphy could be president. Avery Dennis could be the fascist dictator of a small country.
Editor's Note: I could easily run a large country. Also, I'd be benevolent.

NATALIE: Luke Murphy is arguably the most popular guy at San Anselmo Prep. But he's different than you'd expect, because he's just so *nice*. Like he does some charity thing with tutoring special-needs kids or helping old people or something. He's really nice. Teachers love him. Students love him. Babies and grandmas probably love him, too. Everybody loves Luke Murphy.

BECCA: I really can't think of anything bad to say about him. Really, the man *should* be president. Especially after what he did to Avery Dennis.

NATALIE: I still can't believe that we were there when it actually happened. Like, *I* was a witness to the Dumping of Avery Dennis. Oh—this is the other thing to know about Avery Dennis. She's never been single. But she's also never been dumped.

BECCA: Oh, I believe that Avery Dennis has never been dumped. Probably because she usually only dates other people with reptile-size brains.

NATALIE: I was sitting in the library with Becca, working on my math homework.

BECCA: I was *not* sitting with Natalie Wagner. We were sitting at the same table. We were *not* sitting together. I just want to make that clear.

NATALIE: Avery Dennis and I have the same free period. So there I was, just casually minding my own business and doing homework. Avery and Luke were sitting at the table next to mine. I could hear her giggling and I think she was, like, kicking him under the table but in like a footsie way, not in like an aggressive way.

BECCA: I wasn't paying attention to Avery Dennis and Luke Murphy, because I am a normal person with homework of my own to attend to. Also, Ms. Dickerson was trying to secretly eat a sandwich at her desk, so I was staring at her. Just to make her uncomfortable.

MS. DICKERSON, *librarian*: I most certainly was not eating a sandwich at my desk. School policy expressly forbids food in the library.
> *Editor's Note: She was most definitely eating a sandwich. It was totally obvious. At least when Ms. Segerson eats Chipotle during class, she owns it. But she never shares.*

NATALIE: And then he started whispering. Then she whispered a little. Then he whispered a lot more. And then there was some furious simultaneous whispering. And then Luke Murphy whispered for a long, long time, and Avery Dennis was silent. Well, she was silent for a while . . .

BECCA: Avery Dennis let out an unholy screech. Like the kind of thing you would hear from a particularly vitriolic demon.

NATALIE: I looked over and she was standing. Her mouth was hanging open like she was still screaming, but no sound came out. The entire library was totally silent—everyone was staring at her in shock. Even Ms. Dickerson didn't come over and yell at her for screaming in the library.

BECCA: At this point, I was looking at them because, hello, she had just screamed her tiny head off.
> *Editor's Note: I have a very normal-size head.*

NATALIE: Luke Murphy started to get up, and said, "Avery, I am so, so, so," but she didn't even let him finish. She screamed again and he sat down really fast and then she kicked her chair, and her foot went right through it. Like right straight through the back of the chair.

BECCA: Which was a really beautiful thing, because then she started hopping around and screaming and she could not get her foot out.

NATALIE: She was so lucky she was wearing pants; otherwise, that chair totally would have stabbed her leg.

BECCA: Luke Murphy said, "Avery, let me help you," then she screamed, "DON'T YOU DARE!"

NATALIE: Luke kind of shrunk down in his seat and looked really, really scared.

BECCA: Ms. Dickerson must have regained her composure, because she whisper-yelled, "Avery Dennis, that is ENOUGH!" And Avery finally stopped screaming. Ms. Dickerson extricated Avery's foot from the chair and escorted her out of the library.

MS. DICKERSON: Completely uncharacteristic behavior. Yes, I have to shush Avery on an almost hourly basis, but she's not the type of student to be purposely disruptive. Or to destroy school property.

NATALIE: As she was leaving, Avery wailed, "I can't believe this happened right before the prom!" It was so sad. I felt really bad for her.

BECCA: It was one of the most amazing things I'd ever seen.

TRIPP GOMEZ-PARKER, *lacrosse teammate of L. Murphy*: I told him not to do it. You don't dump girls like Avery Dennis, man. You just don't do it. But Luke's got this, like, wacko sense of ethics or whatever. Said he couldn't keep dating her if he didn't feel it. It wouldn't be fair. Like he was lying to her or something. Man, that kid is crazy. Like going to the prom with a hot girl is such a moral dilemma. You think Coco Kim is my soul mate? No. But she's gonna look bangin' in our prom photos. Just suck it up and rent the tux like the rest of us.

NATALIE: I don't even remember how I figured out exactly what had happened. Everything happened so fast.

BECCA: It was obvious what had happened. Why? Because I understand context clues. 1. Luke Murphy whispered a bunch of stuff. 2. Avery Dennis screamed like a deranged banshee and had a complete meltdown. 3. Avery Dennis said something about the prom.

NATALIE: Within minutes, it was all over the school. Everyone knew that Avery Dennis had been dumped. And only days before the prom. I'm only a freshman—I wasn't even going to prom—and *I* was freaking out! Legit everyone was freaking out. How could *Avery Dennis* have been dumped? And how could *Avery Dennis* not have a prom date?! It didn't make sense. Nothing made sense anymore. It was like we'd all just seen a zebra eat a lion. The world had lost its natural order.

BECCA: Everyone knew. But I didn't understand why everyone *cared*.

TRIPP: No, I wasn't there when it happened. But I knew it was *gonna* happen. So I wasn't surprised when I heard about it.

> *Editor's Note: A little heads-up would have been nice, Tripp. We were in the same discussion group in English third quarter. DID THAT MEAN NOTHING TO YOU?!*

NATALIE: The ramifications of this entire situation were immediately obvious. Avery Dennis no longer had a boyfriend. So she no longer had a prom date. And *every* single upperclassman already had a date to the prom. Well, except the people who weren't going to prom. But, like, who doesn't go to prom?

BECCA: Smart people don't go to prom. Luke Murphy had just done Avery Dennis a favor.

NATALIE: San Anselmo Prep was just too small. There were no prom dates left. What was Avery going to do, take a *freshman* to prom? Please. The shame! She was literally out of options. The head of the Prom Committee didn't have a date to prom. And *that* was irony.

PROM COMMITTEE,
PART ONE

AVERY: Needless to say, when I arrived at Prom Committee after a *very* lengthy discussion with Principal Patel, I was strongly considering running away instead of running Prom Committee. And who could blame me, after getting detention *and* a bill for a new library chair? Dad was going to be *thrilled* about that one.

COCO KIM, *best friend:* Poor Avery. I knew what had just happened—practically the minute her foot went through the chair, the entire school knew Luke Murphy had dumped her. Even in Prom Committee, everyone had been talking about it literally right up until the minute Avery walked through the door. I felt so bad for her. But with my best-friend intuition, I knew the last thing she would want was for anyone to feel bad for her. So I just nodded at her super casually yet regally, like I was Eunice Kennedy welcoming Jackie back to Hyannis Port. Avery was wearing sunglasses indoors. It seemed like a very Jackie move.

AVERY: I didn't want anyone to see my eyes! No one at this school had EVER seen Avery Dennis cry, and I wasn't about to let them start! I would much rather be known as the girl who kicked her foot through a chair than the girl who cried over Luke Murphy. I couldn't believe I had lost my cool like that. And over a *guy*, of all things. Beyond embarrassing.

COCO: "One must not let oneself be overwhelmed by sadness." Jacqueline Kennedy Onassis. I think a Kennedy documentary or two could have been very helpful to Avery's life at the moment. Or to anyone's life at any moment, really.
   Editor's Note: Sometimes I felt like Coco and Ms. Segerson were colluding to get me more interested in history. It wasn't going to happen.

BIZZY STANHOPE, *officially the worst*: Poor, poor Avery Dennis. Oh, how the mighty have fallen.
   Editor's Note: Bizzy Stanhope and I have been mortal enemies since kindergarten. Since San Anselmo Prep is a K–12 school, I have unfortunately been stuck with her ever since.

COCO: God, I hate Bizzy Stanhope. Back when we were in kindergarten, she told everyone my lunch smelled weird on the first day of school. But Avery had my back. She spent the remainder of the day quietly filling up Bizzy's shoes with glitter. We'd been in our socks since naptime. When Bizzy went to put her shoes on and leave for the day, she ended up with the shiniest socks ever. When she got home and took her shoes off, it was a glitter explosion. Have you ever tried to clean up glitter? There's probably still some flakes under her couch.

AVERY: And best of all, I never got caught. Sure, Bizzy *tried* to tell the teacher it was me, but she had no proof. Even in kindergarten, I was just that good. The Glitter Bandit of San Anselmo Prep remains at large.

COCO: Just one of many wonderful episodes in a long and beautiful best-friendship.

AVERY: I just wish Prom Committee wasn't a volunteer activity. I would have drummed Bizzy Stanhope's ass out long ago if I could have.

BIZZY: I felt terrible for Avery. When she walked into Prom Committee, it was immediately obvious that she was distraught.
Editor's Note: It was NOT obvious. Because of the sunglasses.

COCO: Avery slid into her customary seat at the head of the table, head held high. But she couldn't even get a word out before Bizzy starting blabbing.

BIZZY: Before we got down to business, I knew there was something that had to be said. I offered to take over as head of the Prom Committee. It was the kind thing to do—no, the *only* thing to do. How could Avery possibly continue on, knowing she was the only person on Prom Committee without a date? It was too, too painful. I couldn't let the poor thing deal with all that trauma.

AVERY: I politely informed Bizzy just exactly where she could stick her offer to oust me from power.

BIZZY: I was *shocked* by her refusal of an offer I'd made out of the goodness of my heart—and, quite frankly, *appalled* by Avery's use of language.

AVERY: I could have said worse. Way worse.

BIZZY: If we're being completely honest, I *should* have been head of the Prom Committee to begin with. After all, I *did* secure the venue. And isn't the venue the most important part of prom?

AVERY: *Secured the venue????* Please. The only thing Bizzy did to secure that venue was to be *born*. Yes, technically, Bizzy did get us the top-floor event space at the B of A building because her dad works at B of A. But she didn't do anything! She just got the venue because of who her dad is. Like, no one congratulates Prince William on getting the British throne just because of who his dad is. Prince William didn't do anything! He deserves no praise! If we're going to praise anyone, let's praise Kate Middleton. She worked *hard* for her title. She persevered through the time they were "on a break" and dealt with the queen constantly throwing her shade. Also, one time at

Nordstrom, I tried on those L.K. Bennett sledge heels she always wears, and they hurt my feet so bad I couldn't walk in them at all. She's done a lot, Kate Middleton.

BIZZY: I told Avery that I just didn't want her to embarrass herself. I was looking out for the poor, pathetic, dateless thing. Can you imagine how mortifying that would be? To be the only single person walking into the prom *alone*? And it just didn't look right for the head of the Prom Committee to not have a date. It was, quite frankly, borderline inappropriate.

COCO: Avery stared down Bizzy from behind her shades. It was a total power move. It was like we were all witnesses to the Cuban Missile Crisis and Avery was John F. Kennedy.
   Editor's Note: Just call her Bizzy Khrushchev. See, Ms. Segerson? I take great notes.

BIZZY: She went totally psycho. Avery started ranting something about single ladies and Taylor Swift and the new millennium. Honestly, I stopped paying attention.

COCO: It was a completely inspirational speech. Then Avery banged her fist on the table and shouted, "To hell with your heteronormative prom industrial complex!"

BIZZY: Naturally, I asked her if that meant she was resigning as head of the Prom Committee.

AVERY: I screamed, "IN YOUR DREAMS, BIZZY!" In hindsight, I could have come up with a more articulate comeback, but that's the problem with comebacks—you can never think up a good one right in the moment.

COCO: Avery informed everyone that she would 110 percent be at prom, date or no date, because she could rock prom just fine on her own, thank you very much. Avery was totally right, and I agreed. She'd go by herself and have the best time. And really, who even needed boys at all!

AVERY: What was so great about a prom date? Bizzy's boyfriend was her prom date, and he doesn't even have a neck!

BIZZY: Sean has a *neck!* It's just very thick because he is so muscular.

AVERY: He legit has no neck.

BIZZY: But since I am a magnanimous person, I simply ignored that insult, took the high road, and wished Avery good luck. Because she was gonna need it. I didn't buy her pathetic "all the single ladies" posturing for one minute. Not have a prom date? Please. That was too tragic, even for a Dennis. No reputable member of Prom Committee would go alone. I knew she'd be desperate to find someone, but there was no way she could. It was way too late. There wasn't an acceptable single man for miles. There was no way Avery was going to find a prom date. And I couldn't wait to see the sad little look on her normally smug, stupid face when she walked into prom totally and completely alone.

AVERY: See? I told you. Bizzy Stanhope was officially the worst.

THE PLAN

AVERY: On the outside, I appeared confident as always. But on the inside, I was in complete and total crisis mode.

COCO: As Kennedy said, "The Chinese use two brushstrokes to write the word *crisis*. One brushstroke stands for danger, the other for opportunity. In a crisis, be aware of the danger—but recognize the opportunity."

Editor's Note: Kennedy really said this, but when you google it, all the results are about this idea being a myth.

AVERY: For once, a Kennedy quote was actually applicable to the situation. I was freaking out . . . but not about prom. Basically, I had two options: Accept defeat, or get creative. And a Dennis *never* accepts defeat.

COCO: Wasn't your mom defeated in the state comptroller election?

AVERY: She insisted on three recounts.

COCO: The apple did not fall far from the tree.

AVERY: Stop asking questions! This is *my* oral history. You're messing with the format!

COCO: The format? The format was to interview your grandma or whatever.

> *Editor's Note: Nowhere in the assignment did it say "interview your grandma."*

AVERY: I knew I had to do something. I was going to be like a Kennedy looking at brushstrokes to find the opportunity in this completely heinous crisis. There had to be an opportunity to learn here, somewhere, right? A reason why the universe had forced me to undergo this horrible trial? I just didn't realize *what* the opportunity was until I was in American history class the next day, and Ms. Segerson started talking about oral history.

MS. SEGERSON: I was talking about the oral history *final project*—to interview several people about an event in American history they had experienced. I doubted that Avery had even started hers.

AVERY: There was no time for homework! My entire reputation was at stake!

MS. SEGERSON: Time for homework? There is always time for homework. There were only two weeks of classes left. Why couldn't the seniors just hold it together?

AVERY: If oral histories could help us understand *why* certain events had happened, then my opportunity was obvious: I needed to conduct my very own oral history. I had been in a lot of relationships—that was incontrovertible fact. But all of those relationships had ended. And yes, I had been the one who ended all of them—except one—but that doesn't change the fact that they *ended*. Why had that happened, time and time again? Was I driven by some sort of destructive force that was dooming me to be forever alone?! There was totally an opportunity here for enlightenment and self-actualization and all those empowering terms on Coco's INSPO Pinterest board. Maybe if I interviewed all of my old boyfriends, the reason why I had ended up single right before the most important "date night" of my life so far would reveal itself to me. Maybe the reason why I *always* ended up single would finally be clear. But most importantly, I hoped these interviews would reveal something about *me*. This would be an epic project, a history on a grand scale, and I would call it . . . "It's Not Me, It's You: An Oral History of Boys."

COCO: When Avery told me she wanted to interview *all* of her old boyfriends, I thought she had lost it. No, I *knew* she had lost it. Avery had *never* been single. Ever. She'd had like four hundred boyfriends!
  Editor's Note: Genius is rarely appreciated in its own time.

AVERY: Coco, although not usually prone to exaggeration, was totally exaggerating. I have not had *that* many boyfriends! But at least she wouldn't have to worry about adding any new ones to the mix. I was one hundred percent completely done with dating until I had my answer. Finished. Over it. I'd spent so much time being someone's girlfriend, I was starting to worry I didn't know how to just be *me*, which was obviously unacceptable. So, no more boyfriends. And no prom date. Because contrary to what Bizzy Stanhope might have you believe, you can absolutely function on your own at a social event. Coco's a better dancer than Luke Murphy anyway.

COCO: I was glad Avery was so chill about going to prom on her own, but she was way *too* relaxed about the immense undertaking ahead of us! How were we supposed to interview *all* of Avery's exes before prom? It was barely two weeks away—it was impossible!

AVERY: Impossible? Audrey Hepburn once said, "Nothing is impossible; the word itself says 'I'm possible!'" Tell JFK to stick that in his pipe and smoke it!

COCO: JFK liked to smoke cigars, but he didn't want to be photographed smoking them.
> *Editor's Note: All appearances to the contrary, this is actually not an oral history of the Kennedys.*

AVERY: I had finally figured it out. When we study the past, we learn more about the present—and more importantly, our future!

MS. SEGERSON: Avery had a very liberal interpretation of the definition of history and its utility. I had recommended several times that she read E. H. Carr's *What Is History?*, but I feared my wishes were falling on deaf ears.

AVERY: I knew the reason why my relationships had never worked would be found somewhere in the past. This is the lesson of *Back to the Future*!

COCO: I didn't understand why she couldn't just ask Luke why he ended things.

AVERY: Luke Murphy *dumped* me. Dumped. Me. He obviously knew nothing. So now I was done with dating. Sorry, boys, you can all blame Luke!

COCO: This sounded crazy—even for Avery. Maybe the Luke breakup sent her into a spin and she *was* just doing this to find a prom date, like in *What's Your Number?* I've seen that film multiple times, because Chris Evans is very frequently shirtless. And the lesson I learned was this: If you've dumped someone once before, chances are, you probably won't want to date them again.

AVERY: I didn't want to date them again! I just wanted to, like, understand my life and the events that had led me to become the person I am today! I'm not doing this to find a prom date. It is for science. Prom will be great because I planned a great prom. End of story.

COCO: After Avery yelled, "THIS IS NOT *WHAT'S YOUR NUMBER?* HOW DARE YOU!" I finally understood that she really didn't care that she had a prom date and that she was "done with dating and am focusing on my career"—her words. Although I'm not totally sure what Avery's career is.

Editor's Note: Obviously, my career is head of the Prom Committee slash student slash future leader of America, thank you very much.

MS. SEGERSON: While I appreciated Avery's enthusiasm for oral history, I felt her energies would be better directed elsewhere. In the grand scheme of things, senior prom really doesn't matter very much.

AVERY: I had the sneaking suspicion Ms. Segerson hadn't even been to her own senior prom.

MS. SEGERSON: I didn't go to prom at my high school. And I turned out fine.

Editor's Note: Did she, though? . . . Did she turn out fine?

COCO: When I finally understood what Avery was going for with her oral history project, I was impressed. It was downright noble! If interviewing all her ex-boyfriends was what Avery needed to be her best self, I would be right there with her to help, every step of the way. Just like I'd helped when she somehow got that ship in her dad's office out of its bottle. We would get Avery's relationships back in the bottle. Wait . . . This metaphor doesn't really work, does it?

AVERY: I couldn't do this alone, though. It wasn't impossible — but as Coco had pointed out, it was a big job. I needed help. And as my dad always says, when you want something done right, you get the best people to do it for you.

HUTCH

AVERY: Hutch was the greatest scientific mind San Anselmo had ever produced. After four years of winning state and regional science fairs, he'd just won a crazy buttload of scholarship money in a national science competition. Most importantly, on the very first day of freshman biology, a stunningly gorgeous but uninterested girl sat next to a new kid known as James "Hutch" Hutcherson, and the two of them became lab partners. That girl . . . was me.

JAMES "HUTCH" HUTCHERSON, *great scientific mind*: That girl was *Avery Dennis*?! I'm shocked. Nobody saw that coming.

CRESSIDA SCHROBENHAUSER-CLONAN, *totally bitter AP bio student*: Yeah, I remember the first day of freshman bio. Hutch was sitting at the lab table closest to the door. Avery Dennis slid in just as the bell was ringing and into the closest available seat—the one next to Hutch.

AVERY: But Hutch actually showed me that science was cool. I was as surprised as *you* probably are right now reading this. And thanks to the classic San Anselmo Prep insistence on student self-advocacy, we have been lab partners every year since. Hutch turned that uninterested freshman girl into a bona fide science whiz who is very much holding her own in AP bio, thank you very much.

CRESSIDA: Every year, every single year, I watched as Hutch and Avery lab-partnered again and again. I couldn't understand it. Was I jealous? Yes. I was beyond jealous. Year after year, I was stuck with a deadweight of a lab partner, dragging me down. This year was the absolute worst. Tripp Gomez-Parker? His brain is protozoan. I have no idea how he made it into AP.

TRIPP GOMEZ-PARKER: Yeah, Hutch is like a guaranteed three-point bump to your GPA. He's a genius, man.

AVERY: Even *I* wondered sometimes why Hutch was still my lab partner. And once I had to go to counseling for having high self-esteem.

HUTCH: I was still Avery's lab partner because, all appearances to the contrary, Avery Dennis doesn't play. She gets it *done*.

CRESSIDA: We all knew why Hutch was still Avery's lab partner. Because she's pretty. That was it, right? That was literally all Avery Dennis brought to the table. Even the smartest boys were dumb about some things.
   Editor's Note: Ouch.

HUTCH: Anybody who wonders why I'd lab-partner AD has never seen her dissect a frog. Steadiest hands I've ever seen.

Minimal, beautiful incisions. Speed and accuracy. She can get the spleen out of anything—mammal or amphibian—in less time than it takes a normal person to tie their shoes.

AVERY: We don't dissect things nearly often enough for that to be a huge advantage, but it's always nice to be appreciated for your skills. And speaking of skills, Hutch had the exact skill set I needed to complete my oral history project. He was the master of deductive reasoning. If anyone was going to discern a pattern here, it was Hutch. He could sift through mountains of data and find exactly what he needed to prove any hypothesis.

HUTCH: When AD first approached me, I thought she'd forgotten a pencil. Like she does. Every. Single. Day.

AVERY: Despite his brilliant mind, he was also, unfortunately, a known slanderer.

HUTCH: This was supposed to be an objective study. A history. I was trying to stick to the facts. As with everything in life, if the data is inaccurate, the results will be inconclusive.

AVERY: He was also almost always right. It was one of his best *and* most annoying characteristics.

HUTCH: Yeah, I am always right. This is exactly why we scientists are a lonely breed.

AVERY: Hutch was an impartial observer, which I felt made him a great objective source for my history. Prom can make people really emotional. It is the single biggest day of our entire lives so far. It is going to be the most magical evening we have literally ever experienced.

TRIPP: I heard Coco's dress is totally backless. This night is gonna be *magical*.
   Editor's Note: Gross. Tripp Gomez-Parker was going to keep his hands where I could see them the entire evening, or he would face the wrath of Avery.

COCO: Avery and I spent weeks picking out the right dresses. Mine is magical.

AVERY: When I think about taking pictures with Coco, riding in a limousine, and walking into the venue I'll have transformed with my own two hands . . . Sure, I get excited about it. But the thing is, when you join the Prom Committee, you're agreeing to throw the best party you can for everyone. It's not just about you, it's about the school. Most people won't thank you for it. The thanks you get are when everyone is out on the dance floor having the time of their lives, possibly for the last time together . . . ugh, I'm getting choked up already. It's going to be amazing. See? Emotional. But I knew Hutch wouldn't get emotional. For one thing, scientists remain impartial. And more importantly, Hutch *couldn't* get emotional. Because he wasn't going to the prom.

HUTCH: Are you kidding me? No, of course I wasn't going to the prom. Why would I spend seventy-five dollars on a ticket to an event I had absolutely no interest in attending? For seventy-five dollars, I could buy multiple expansion packs for Ticket to Ride. I'd had my eye on that Southeast Asian expansion pack for quite some time. I was not about to blow the graduation money from my grandma on a prom ticket. Not to mention the tux and any other hidden expenses prom might incur.

    Editor's Note: Ticket to Ride is a board game in which you build train tracks? Unclear.

CRESSIDA: I knew Hutch wasn't going to prom. Lucky him. So now I had absolutely no reason whatsoever to go. Not that Hutch is a *reason* for me to go to the prom; it would just be nice to have one person there with whom one could have an intelligent conversation, besides the chaperones.

HUTCH: Besides, prom is stupid. I don't dress up on Halloween, and I don't dress up for dances. Also, I don't dance.

    Editor's Note: WHY DIDN'T HE WEAR HALLOWEEN COSTUMES?! WHAT WAS WRONG WITH HIM?! This was something that needed to be addressed at a later date, clearly.

AVERY: Hutch didn't seem to understand. The senior prom is literally a once-in-a-lifetime event. It'll never happen again. It's not like prom is a trip to In-N-Out. Animal fries are forever, but prom is one night only.

Editor's Note: For the uninitiated, animal fries are cheesy fries smothered in In-N-Out Burger's secret sauce and sautéed onions. They are nature's perfect food.

HUTCH: Whether or not prom was stupid was a moot point. I didn't have a prom ticket. I wasn't going to prom. More importantly, I had alternate plans.

AVERY: I was surprised Hutch had alternate prom night plans. Until I found out what they were. And then I wasn't surprised at all.

HUTCH: We start the evening off with a game of my own devising, Settlers of Ca-Tots. It's basically Catan, except the only viable trade resource is tater tots.

MICHAEL FEELEY, *member of Hutch's Dragon Wizarding Warlord Association or whatever*: My mom already stocked up on tots with her Costco membership. The backup freezer in our garage is literally full of tots right now. Nothing. But. Tots.

HUTCH: So we keep things light in the early part of the evening. Ca-Tots, then Lords of Waterdeep, then Dust. But that's only the beginning.

LIAM PADALECKI, *another member of Hutch's Dragon Wizarding Warlord Association or whatever*: Exactly at the stroke of midnight, we begin Dungeons & Dragons: The Rise of Tiamat. And then we rage 'til *dawn*!

HUTCH: I had been planning this campaign for more than a semester. These guys are gonna get *destroyed*.

LIAM: It's so cute how Hutch thinks he's gonna wreck us. No way, man. No way. This is gonna be *easy*. People always under-estimate a tiefling bard. That's our secret.

MICHAEL: Liam said what? Ugh. Typical tiefling nonsense. He needs to take this *seriously*. Hutch is gonna bring his A-game. He always does. Man, we probably *are* gonna get crushed. Our campaign has like five bards right now. It's nonsense. But no one ever listens to the gnome.

HUTCH: Tiamat is a dragon, AD. It does not get cooler than that. Is prom gonna have dragons? Or devastation orbs?

> *Editor's Note: Who would want to go to any event that had something called a devastation orb?? Generally speaking, I try to avoid devastation, no matter what its geometric shape, in my daily life.*

AVERY: Clearly, I had missed out on a great theme idea: Dragons under the Stars. I don't know what I'd been thinking when I selected Midnight in Paris. Even though that was technically a misnomer, since prom ended promptly—and tragically—at 11:00 p.m.

HUTCH: Prom might end at eleven, but at Ultimate Game Night, we rage until dawn.

Editor's Note: Rage was definitely not the verb he was looking for.

MICHAEL: Oh, we were gonna rage, all right. My mom got so much Mountain Dew at Costco I could build a fort out of it. Nobody sleeps at Ultimate Game Night!

HUTCH: Clearly, AD had never been on a campaign with me as the Dungeon Master.

Editor's Note: The only campaign I've ever been on was when my mom ran for state comptroller, and that was plenty boring.

AVERY: If my oral history had been a lab report, Hutch never would have gotten so off task.

HUTCH: Fine. She wants a lab report? Does this whacked-out project even have a hypothesis?

AVERY: If I interview all my old boyfriends, then I will find out what went wrong. I'll find out why I was dumped mere days before the most important night of my life—senior prom. I'll figure out *why* all of my relationships ended—and what, exactly, that says about me. Which will totally help me in my new life as a single college freshman who is not distracted by dating at all and is way too busy having an obscenely high GPA and running the Student Government Association to waste any time on a boyfriend. Simple.

HUTCH: Nothing about this "history" included a hypothesis that was remotely testable.

AVERY: That's why it's a history project! Not a science project!

HUTCH: Is this even an oral history? You're seriously screwing with the format.

AVERY: *You're* screwing with the format! You're not supposed to talk to me! I mean, you are, but I'm just supposed to be like an impartial observer!

HUTCH: You have never been an impartial observer of anything in your entire life.
   Editor's Note: Fact.

AVERY: Please help me! Please please please please please!

HUTCH: Chill, AD! You know you annoy people until they have no choice but to do your bidding, right?

AVERY: It's an effective technique.

HUTCH: I will help you, but only for science. Because this is the most whacked-out hypothesis I've ever heard. Which means I'm probably the only person in San Anselmo who could prove it.

AVERY: And that was exactly why I'd asked Hutch for his help. Unfortunately, Hutch wasn't available for step one of the project.

HUTCH: *Discover* was doing an article on teens in science.

AVERY: Hey! You should tell them about my oral history! It's a totally unusual hypothesis, just like you said, right? I bet *Discover* would be totally into it.

HUTCH: I am absolutely not doing that.

AVERY: Fine. I'll call *Discover* and tell them about it myself when it's finished.

HUTCH: So *Discover* had asked to profile me for this article. And normally my reaction to getting my picture taken for anything was no—

AVERY: You are on the cover of literally every single piece of promotional material at San Anselmo Prep.

HUTCH: I didn't know they were taking those pictures.

AVERY: Sure, somebody walks into a classroom, holding a camera, but your nose is too deep in A *Brief History of Time* to notice a flash.

HUTCH: I can't help that I have the photogenic complexion and charisma of a young Neil deGrasse Tyson.

AVERY: The San Anselmo Prep admissions team does love a nice, diverse picture. If you looked at our brochures, you'd think Hutch and Coco were in every class together.

HUTCH: But it was *Discover*, man! I had to say yes. I still couldn't believe I was going to be in those hallowed pages. Just like Neil deGrasse Tyson and Dennis Bray and Alain Aspect and—

AVERY: You're just making up words now.

HUTCH: They're scientists, AD.

AVERY: Whatever. Hutch was off to be America's Next Top Model Scientist—

HUTCH: How do you not know who Neil deGrasse Tyson is? He's like the Drake of the scientific community! It's like you don't even listen to me.

AVERY: Fine! Hutch was off to be the next Neil deGrasse Tyson. Which meant I needed assistance from elsewhere. Luckily, I knew exactly who to turn to—the person who had been by my side when it all began. The witness to the very first case in my oral history—my best friend, Coco Kim.

BOBBY BOBACK

AVERY: My first boyfriend wasn't my boyfriend. He was . . . my husband.

COCO: Dramatic much? You're sensationalizing, child bride.

AVERY: I'm trying to pull in the reader!

COCO: The reader? Who's reading this?

AVERY: The historical record.

COCO: Oh, boy.

AVERY: *I'm* asking the questions here, Coco! Just answer them, please.

COCO: Avery and I have been best friends since before we were even born. There are pictures of our moms posing together, showing off their completely chic baby bumps. So I was well versed in the histrionic language of Avery.
Editor's Note: People probably called Shakespeare histrionic, too, and look at how well things turned out for him.

COCO: *Of course* I was there for Avery's first boyfriend. I've been there for almost every single boyfriend! Well, most of the ones that she met in the contiguous United States, anyway.

Editor's Note: Those other boyfriends were going to be hard to track down . . . OR WERE THEY??? Look at the foreshadowing, Ms. Segerson! I'm pulling in the reader!

COCO: Anyway, we didn't need to worry about any of Avery's other boyfriends just yet. We were talking about Bobby Boback, Boyfriend #1.

AVERY: Bobby was cute. So cute. Crazy cute. Like he should have had his own show on the Disney Channel cute.

COCO: We all noticed him right away. How could we not? He was *adorable*. Big brown eyes, a shock of hair always falling across his face . . . I mean, who wouldn't want to put their nap mat down next to that. Amiright? I was so excited to call Bobby again. I was sure he was still just as cute! Not that we'd be able to tell how cute he was over the phone, but still. It was exciting.

BOBBY BOBACK, *Boyfriend #1:* Oh, man. Wow. Avery Dennis. Before Coco and Avery called me, I hadn't heard that name in a long time. She had really, really long, really blond hair, right? That's about all I remember.

AVERY: Some might say kindergarten is early to start a relationship, but I was an advanced child.

BOBBY: Wait a minute—Avery Dennis? You're saying she was my girlfriend? You're sure about that?

AVERY: HE DOESN'T REMEMBER ME????

COCO: He was absolutely Avery's boyfriend. I remember. Because we had just had snack, and Avery marched up to him and said, "You're my boyfriend now," and he said, "Okay," and then at recess Avery said, "We're getting married now," and he said, "Okay," and I remember this *very* well because I officiated the ceremony.

BOBBY: Man, I don't remember any of this.

AVERY: THIS IS WHY MY RELATIONSHIPS NEVER WORK OUT. BECAUSE I AM COMPLETELY AND UTTERLY FORGETTABLE!!!

BOBBY: If you say I dated Avery Dennis, I believe you. I just don't remember it. My memories from back when we lived in California are super fuzzy.

COCO: Seriously? I can't believe you don't remember this! Honestly, Bobby, this was a total waste of a phone call to Michigan.

BOBBY: It's, uh, Rob now.

AVERY: NOBODY ASKED YOU, BOBBY.

COCO: Don't worry, Avery, *I* remember what happened. Avery and Bobby were married until the end of the day, then Avery dumped him right before she went home, and he said, "Okay." It was pretty amicable, all things considered.

BOBBY: Uh, okay.

AVERY: *Plus ça change, plus ç'est la même chose,* Bobby.

BOBBY: Rob.

AVERY: GET OUT!

BOBBY: *YOU* called *ME!*
   Editor's Note: He hung up.

AVERY: This was a total disaster. My oral history project was a complete and utter failure. Boyfriend #1 didn't even remember me! I learned absolutely nothing about *why* I'm single right now or about why I *always* end up single—before I start going out with someone new, anyway. How could I be expected to break this endless pattern of doomed relationships if I didn't even know *why* they were doomed?

COCO: I realized our mistake immediately. We weren't going to learn *anything* exploring these deep cuts. The answer was obvious: We needed to fast-forward a couple years. It was time to reconnect with Avery's first *real* boyfriend. The first one she kissed.

AVERY: She had a point—and it was certainly more efficient than lingering in the K–5 years. But I wasn't sure I was ready for where she wanted to go. I had, after all, been recently dumped. The wounds were still fresh.

COCO: Fasten your seat belts, it's going to be a bumpy night—we're going back to middle school.

Editor's Note: I am probably the only person in the history of time who looked cute in her seventh-grade school photo. And I was still nervous about revisiting middle school. Rough times, man.

ROBBY MONROE

COCO: First Bobby? Now Robby? For the first time, I realized Avery had a serious Robert problem.

> *Editor's Note: Robert is a very noble name! It literally means "bright with glory." BRIGHT WITH GLORY. Who doesn't want a boyfriend who's bright with glory? Also, since Robby still went to our school, I knew I didn't have to contend with him being all pissy about only being called Rob now. Some men have the confidence to keep rocking the Robby.*

AVERY: Robby was new in sixth grade. I spotted him and his immaculate calves immediately on the first day of school. God, I love the first day of school. Always new boys. That is probably the worst thing about going to a small school—the boys get totally stale.

HUTCH: I had no idea why Avery and Coco wanted me to be part of this Robby Monroe interview—I didn't even go to San Anselmo Prep in sixth grade.

> *Editor's Note: He was there to analyze the evidence, DUH!!!! Honestly, sometimes I swear it's like Hutch doesn't even listen to me. I'd have to cover my body in, like, constellations or microspores or something if I wanted him to actually pay attention to me.*

BIZZY STANHOPE, *officially the worst*: Yeah, I guess Robby Monroe was cute in sixth grade. In a generic way. Like, that was exactly the kind of nondescript person Avery would set her sights on. No offense! I mean, he was totally good for *Avery*.

Editor's Note: Offense!!! I take offense!!

COCO: There was a general buzzing amongst us sixth-grade girls about new Robby being cute, but it wasn't until the soccer season started that Robby was, like, a *thing*.

BIZZY: Robby's good at something, right? Like some sport or something? I'm sorry, I'm so busy with Sean during football season, I just don't know what else goes on in the fall.

Editor's Note: Oh my God, the only team sports San Anselmo Prep offers guys in the fall are football and soccer. There are literally ONLY TWO THINGS.

AVERY: He was *amazing*. I was on the swing set with Coco after school one day when I saw Robby dribbling down the field.

COCO: I am an avowed sports hater, but the first time I saw Robby play, even I was impressed.

TRIPP GOMEZ-PARKER, *soccer teammate of R. Monroe*: Robby carries the team, man. And he has since sixth grade. Definitely the best forward we have. I think Coach started crying when Robby showed up.

COACH BRACKETT, *soccer coach:* I have cried only two times in my life: when I watched the US win the World Cup live, and when my daughter was born. So, no, I did not cry when Monroe showed up to tryouts for the first time. Heck of a player, though.

Editor's Note: I swear, though, he looked a little teary just thinking about it.

COCO: So we were sitting on the swing set, but we had both stopped like mid-swing, just staring at Robby with our mouths open. He did this super kick and the ball soared into the net—is it a net? The goal? The goal net? Whatever. And Avery said, I'll never forget it . . .

AVERY: "Coco, I am going to kiss that boy."

COCO: And I knew she would. Avery makes things happen. She's the only person I know who does exactly what she says she's going to do. If Avery said, "Coco, I am going to the moon," I would fully expect her next text to be a space-suit selfie.

Editor's Note: Awww. I <3 Coco. There is nothing better than a best friend who believes in you. Would I go to the moon? Depends on if they've improved on that nasty space ice cream, I think.

HUTCH: I see our first pattern emerging already: Avery as aggressor. Not that I'm surprised. All of these relationships have been instigated by Avery.

Editor's Note: Well, he's not wrong, but I don't love the idea of myself as an aggressor. It makes me sound like the Terminator or Predator or some other kind of alien robot monster.

COCO: But Avery didn't make her move on the soccer field. She waited 'til Cressida Schrobenhauser-Clonan's birthday party. Ohh, I *miss* Cressida's birthday parties! Why did Cressida stop having them? They were *so fun.* The whole grade was there and her mom always got ice-cream cake, which is my favorite.

CRESSIDA SCHROBENHAUSER-CLONAN, *AP bio classmate*: Sixth grade was the last year my mom made me have a birthday party. And she made me invite the whole. Freaking. Grade.

BIZZY, *officially the worst*: Oh, yeah, I remember Cressida's birthday parties. They were so *cute.* Like, her mom would actually get balloons and streamers and an ice-cream cake, like it was a birthday party from the 1950s or something. For my sixth-grade birthday, the theme was Cirque du Soleil. Daddy got aerialists, and they were totally amaze.

Editor's Note: Literally no one cares, Bizzy. No one asked about your stupid sixth-grade birthday party. Ugh.

COCO: Because sixth graders couldn't go to the middle school homecoming dance—so rude—Cressida's birthday party was pretty much *the* social event of the fall. Avery and I got ready together, and we spent *so long* on our outfits. And making plans about how Avery could get Robby to kiss her.

AVERY: I was hoping the potent combination of soda and ice-cream cake would create the kind of free-for-all environment where anything could happen.

HUTCH: I almost feel bad for poor Robby Monroe of the past. Avery and Coco plotting about how to get him to smash his face on Avery's sounds like a terrifying prospect.
  Editor's Note: OMG, I am not *terrifying! I swear, Robby was* thrifling *to kiss me. Read on, Hutch. You'll see.*

COCO: Avery had rejected all of the ploys I'd learned from TV—Truth or Dare, Spin the Bottle, etc. Honestly, it was sort of like the blind leading the blind, since I'd never kissed anybody either.

AVERY: I wanted the kiss to happen *naturally*, not because he was forced to kiss me by the laws of Truth or Dare.

HUTCH: Truth or Dare is in no way legally binding.
  Editor's Note: It absolutely is.

ROBBY MONROE, *ex-boyfriend, kind of a big deal on the soccer field*: God, yeah, of course I remember Cressida

Schrobenhauser-Clonan's sixth-grade birthday party. How could I not? That was my first kiss.

Editor's Note: Awww, he remembers! Take that, stupid Bobby Boback!

BIZZY: Um, no, I do not remember what Robby Monroe was doing at Cressida Schrobenhauser-Clonan's sixth-grade birthday party. Tamsin and I were busy secretly opening all of her presents to see if she got anything good. She didn't.

Editor's Note: See? She is a psychopath! Who opens somebody else's birthday presents?!

ROBBY: Sixth grade was rough, man. It's hard being the new kid at a school where everyone's known each other since kindergarten. I had the guys on my team, but I didn't know them that well yet. And of course my mom had dropped me off at the party the minute it started, and no one I knew super well was there yet. Man, I would not repeat middle school for a million dollars. Standing in the corner of Cressida's basement, drinking a Sprite alone, looking around for someone to talk to . . . That was probably the most awkward I've ever felt in my life.

COCO: I *loved* Cressida's basement! It had that big leather sectional that was *so* comfy and a foosball table and Ping-Pong and a nice squashy carpet, and her mom like *never* bothered us. Seriously, someone needs to tell Cressida to start having birthday parties again.

CRESSIDA: I was up in my room, reading. My mom said I had to have a birthday party. She never said I had to be in the room where the party was happening.

ROBBY: I was trying to decide if I should call my mom to come pick me up—or if I could just somehow will myself to disappear into the floor—when the most perfect girl I'd ever seen walked down the stairs to the basement and straight toward me.
  Editor's Note: Perfect?!?! OMG, why did I ever break up with this kid?

COCO: When I walked into the party, I looked behind me and Avery was gone. She'd already gone to find Robby!

ROBBY: I knew who Avery was, of course. She was so confident, so self-assured. She breezed through the hallways like she just couldn't be bothered, like she was somehow immune to middle school. And I couldn't believe she was walking toward me.

AVERY: I was so nervous I was legit shaking. But I guess he had no idea, so go, me.

COCO: I moved toward the foosball table, trying not to be obvious, but completely staring at what I knew was about to happen. Conner Plechaty tried to talk to me, but I totally shushed him. I needed to see what was happening.

Editor's Note: Conner Plechaty kissed Coco like twenty minutes later. I tell you, that basement was magical!

ROBBY: She held out her hand. Her glittery nail polish glinted in the basement light.
Editor's Note: He is like a poet. WHY DID I BREAK UP WITH HIM!?!

AVERY: I said, "Wanna go outside?" and tossed my hair back and forth a few times for good measure.

ROBBY: I would have followed her anywhere. Avery Dennis saved me, man. She saved me from my middle school awkward self.

HUTCH: I was seriously concerned that this whole interview was going to give AD some kind of hero-savior complex.
Editor's Note: When Hutch saved that irregular species of Northern California bee, I was happy for him. You'd think he'd at least extend me and Robby Monroe the same courtesy.

COCO: Avery led Robby through the sliding glass doors and into the backyard. I couldn't believe she had just grabbed his hand and now their fingers were totally intertwined! It was so boss. Conner Plechaty still would not shut up. I stepped on his foot.
Editor's Note: I guess he liked it, because later on, they tooootally kissed. Hahahaha!

ROBBY: There was an old swing set in Cressida's backyard. Avery dropped my hand and sat on one of the swings.

Editor's Note: What is with me and Robby Monroe and swing sets? Is this, like, a leitmotif?

CRESSIDA: A leitmotif is a recurrent theme usually associated with a particular person, place, or idea. Why do you ask?

Editor's Note: So the swing set was totally a leitmotif. The leitmotif representing me and Robby Monroe, the one that got away.

HUTCH: Real life doesn't have leitmotifs. They only exist in works of fiction. Why?

Editor's Note: Sheesh, can't a girl just ask a few casual questions about leitmotifs?

ROBBY: I didn't know what else to do, so I sat down on the swing next to her. I still had that stupid can of Sprite. The condensation on the outside was sweating, or maybe I was sweating. Yeah, I was probably so scared I was sweating.

AVERY: We swung back and forth quietly. I was desperate for him to make a move. I was so scared he *wouldn't* make a move, and then I'd just be an idiot on a swing set. I said I would kiss Robby Monroe, and I knew I wanted to.

ROBBY: I knew I had to say something, but I had no idea what I should say.

AVERY: The silence was killing me. The pressure! The romantic tension! So I just blurted out, "Are you gonna kiss me, or what?"

HUTCH: If you had bet me fifty dollars that I couldn't tell you the story of Avery's first kiss, I would have won. Because that is exactly what I would have guessed.

ROBBY: Now I *really* didn't know what to say. Did I want to kiss her? Are you kidding? Avery Dennis was the prettiest girl I'd ever seen in real life.
   Editor's Note: Ha! See, Hutch? He totally liked me.

AVERY: He started leaning. Which I felt like meant he was going to kiss me. So I closed my eyes and leaned in.

ROBBY: I was sweating so much. I was terrified I had lip sweat.

AVERY: Robby Monroe absolutely did not have lip sweat.

ROBBY: As first kisses go, it wasn't too bad. At least, I didn't think so.
   Editor's Note: It absolutely wasn't too bad at all. Seriously, why did I break up with this guy?

COCO: I saw the whole thing through the glass doors! It was so cute. An old swing set?! It was totally romantic.

CRESSIDA: No, I didn't know that Avery and Robby kissed at my birthday party. But I'm not surprised. No one is safe from the lips of Avery Dennis.

Editor's Note: Guess she was still kind of upset about that thing with her brother . . . but that was a whole different boyfriend altogether. We will deal with Ben when the time comes.

ROBBY: And then, because I was not smooth at all, I immediately asked her to be my girlfriend. Thank God she said yes. We walked back into the party holding hands, and I finally felt like I belonged at San Anselmo Prep.

HUTCH: So Robby asked Avery out. Interesting. But I still think Avery was the major instigator of this relationship. And I bet she instigated ending it, too.

COCO: You know what? I have no idea why Robby and Avery broke up. I can't remember! That is so weird.

Editor's Note: Probably because she was busy eating Conner Plechaty's face, like she was for most of sixth grade.

ROBBY: Yeah, Avery dumped me. We'd been going out for almost the whole year, which is pretty much an eternity in middle school. She said she couldn't be tied down over the summer.

Editor's Note: What. An. Idiot. But who amongst us is wise in middle school?

COCO: She was convinced she was going to meet a hot boy at camp. Well, she wasn't wrong.

HUTCH: Maybe this is the inciting incident in all of Avery's breakups—the eternal search for the better boyfriend? We're going to need more research. This is far too small of a sample size to produce any kind of conclusive finding.

ROBBY: Oh, God, no, no hard feelings. I was crushed for like two minutes and then Tamsin Brewer asked me out.
  Editor's Note: Tamsin Brewer is Bizzy Stanhope's best friend. Questionable taste, Robby.

BIZZY: It was totally Tamsin who *made* Robby. Seriously, no one cared who he was while he was dating Avery. But as soon as he started dating Tamsin, he was hot.
  Editor's Note: Tamsin Brewer couldn't "make" a person. I doubted she could make a Popsicle-stick picture frame.

ROBBY: I will forever be grateful to Avery. She put me on the map at San Anselmo, man. She made me feel like I belonged.

COCO: As much as any two awkward sixth graders can be a cute couple, they were totally a cute couple.

ROBBY: I didn't believe it at first when I heard that Avery was going to the prom alone. That seems like a lonely thing to do.

AVERY: How can you be lonely surrounded by basically all of your best friends, singing and dancing and eating your face off? These prom-date-obsessed people need to get real.

COCO: You know what? After we talked to Robby, I was seriously confused. Not because of anything Robby had said, but because of Avery. Why had she been nervous at all about looking into middle school? Robby was a totally respectable first kiss. Okay, yes, he was a little boring and obsessed with soccer, but he was cute in sixth grade, and he was still cute now. There was even a certain Kennedy-esque quality about the shwoop of his brown hair.

Editor's Note: Only Coco would think a legitimately ancient hairstyle was a plus.

AVERY: Coco had clearly forgotten what was coming down the road. But at least the summer after sixth grade was anything *but* a disaster.

CAMP KAWAWA CHARLIE

AVERY: Camp Kawawa was the closest thing to heaven on earth.

CRESSIDA SCHROBENHAUSER-CLONAN: Camp Kawawa was the lost tenth circle of Dante's *Inferno*. Just when I thought I'd finally gotten away from all the nightmare drones I was forced to interact with in school, guess who was the first person I saw at Camp Kawawa, sitting on top of a picnic table like she owned the place. Avery. Freaking. Dennis.

AVERY: I missed Coco terribly, of course. But there were so many new friends to make! And new boys to kiss! And oh, yeah, Cressida was there, too.

CRESSIDA: I didn't even want to go to sleepaway camp, okay? I wanted to spend the summer reading in my room! But my mom made me.

COCO: I would have loved to go to Camp Kawawa, believe me. But my mom is convinced sleepaway camps are nothing but expensive breeding grounds for bedbugs and lice.

CRESSIDA: Did I have a camp boyfriend? Hilarious. No. I ate lunch with the counselors every day and faked a horse dander allergy.

HUTCH: I googled Kawawa—it means "pitiful" in Tagalog. Clearly a case of unfortunate cultural appropriation. What kind of camp was this?

> *Editor's Note: An awesome camp, Hutch, okay?! We can't all have gone to Space Camp for nine years in a row. And I really doubt that Space Camp had the same wide variety of paste-based arts and crafts that Camp Kawawa did.*

AVERY: I knew talking to my camp boyfriend was going to bring on extreme clarity, because Charlie was basically three boyfriends in one. He'd been my boyfriend every single summer I went to Camp Kawawa—until ninth grade, when my dad declared that summers were for internships or competitions. Unfortunately, I didn't exactly know Charlie's last name. But it turned out, I didn't need to worry—all his contact information was on the Camp Kawawa website. All these years later, he was *still* going to Camp Kawawa. I mean, he wasn't a camper anymore, he was a counselor now—but still.

CHARLIE "CAMP KAWAWA" KASPEROWICZ, *ex-boyfriend, professional camp counselor*: Oh, yeah, Avery Dennis! I remember her. She was my first camp girlfriend.

> *Editor's Note: First?! Not only?! There were others?!*

CRESSIDA: I only went to Camp Kawawa that one summer. Once was more than enough. You would have thought Avery could have bothered to say hi, or ask me to sit with her, or something. We weren't friends at San Anselmo Prep, but we were in a strange environment and we knew only each other. That should have counted for something! But no, she was too busy making goo-goo eyes at Cute Charlie all summer to pay any attention to me.

Editor's Note: OMG, did people call him Cute Charlie?! You go, middle school Avery! Although I did feel bad about not being nicer to Cressida at camp. I thought she liked sitting with the counselors because she appreciated their more mature intellectual ceiling. She was always complaining that there was no one in her cabin who was familiar with Proust.

CHARLIE: I saw Avery sitting on the picnic table on the very first day of camp. That blond hair, it's hard to miss. I just asked her to be my girlfriend, and we fell into the same pattern every year she was there.

HUTCH: So AD didn't initiate this relationship? Well. There goes my whole hypothesis.

CRESSIDA: Once I saw them kiss in a canoe, and I threw up. But then I got out of swimming for the whole day, so I guess it was a win.

COCO: All of Avery's letters home were full of Charlie, Charlie, Charlie. He sounded seriously adorable. Once she tried to draw a portrait. It bore a striking resemblance to the red M&M, but with hair. But when I finally saw a picture, it confirmed my suspicions—he was seriously cute and looked nothing like an M&M.

AVERY: Charlie is so much of my memories of Camp Kawawa, they're inextricable. Canoeing and archery and bonfires and holding hands and Charlie, Charlie, Charlie. Just that total summer feeling of freedom, you know? Maybe I should have tried to make it work. Although what middle schooler could make a long-distance relationship work?

CHARLIE: Do I still have a camp girlfriend? Ha-ha, we don't really call it that anymore. But if Rowan comes back to work at Kawawa . . . yeah, I'd be interested.
   Editor's Note: Coco must find this Rowan person on Facebook immediately. And find out if she's blond. And prettier than me.

CRESSIDA: I remember the last day of camp. You'd have thought Cute Charlie was leaving for the first manned mission to Mars. Avery was weeping into his shirt like he'd abandoned her for the red planet.

CHARLIE: Why'd we break up? Same reason every year. She dumped me because camp was over, but I wasn't too bummed.

Camp relationships are just that—camp relationships. You go into them knowing they'll end. And in some cases, start up again the next year. Or end forever. It's all good.

AVERY: Charlie wasn't wrong, but he wasn't exactly helping me, either. Clearly, Luke Murphy hadn't . . . ugh . . . *dumped* me because of geographic complications. It's not like he ended things just because the school year was ending. If *that* was his reason, he could have waited until after prom like any normal person who goes off to college well aware that long distance is the wrong distance. I was feeling remarkably over the whole Luke Murphy situation, all things considered, but I was still confused about *why* he'd dumped me. And I *hate* feeling confused. It's why I write such clear lab reports.

HUTCH: I've said it before and I'll say it again: AD's lab reports are of a professional caliber. You should see her data tables.

AVERY: At the risk of sounding like Hutch, I wondered what we'd learned from Camp Kawawa Charlie, then, if he broke my pattern.

HUTCH: I was pretty sure I knew what the lesson of Camp Kawawa Charlie was—that it's really easy to be in a relationship when you're basically on vacation and doing nothing but swimming and eating marshmallows all day. It's when real life happens that relationships get complicated.

AVERY: Speaking of complicated, it was time to move on to seventh grade.

LIAM PADALECKI

COCO: If Charlie was the hottest thing at Camp Kawawa since toasted s'mores, why was Avery so embarrassed about her middle school dating history?

AVERY: Coco had clearly blocked my seventh-grade boyfriend out of her generous, kind, self-selecting best-friend memory. But I hadn't forgotten. I *couldn't* forget.

COCO: Avery's boyfriend in seventh grade . . . ? Wait. Shut up. Oh my God. Avery dated Liam Padalecki. Liam Padalecki!! I had totally and completely forgotten.

BIZZY STANHOPE [*evil, maniacal laughter*]: Of *course* I remember when Avery dated Liam Padalecki. The two of them are perfect for each other.

HUTCH: I wasn't even *there*, and I've never forgotten about the Avery and Liam thing. And Liam's never let us forget it either.

LIAM PADALECKI, *ex-boyfriend/Wizarding Warlock*: For about two weeks in seventh grade, I was a straight-up baller.

MICHAEL FEELEY, *Wizarding Warlock*: For about two weeks in seventh grade, Liam was a straight-up jackass. Correction: more of a jackass than usual.

HUTCH: One of the many blessings in my life was the fact that I didn't start at San Anselmo Prep until ninth grade—which means that I had the great good fortune of missing Avery and Liam's "relationship." It was less fortunate, however, that she insisted I come with her to Liam's house so she could interrogate me and all of my friends.

> *Editor's Note: It was going to be a lot more awkward for me than it was for Hutch, but I figured if I could interview Bizzy, I could handle talking to Liam again.*

AVERY: I was confused, okay? It was a weird time. I missed Charlie, and then coming back home from Camp Kawawa was making me miss Robby, and I was just sad about all of it.

COCO: Avery was seriously mopey when she got home. Avery, I love you, but if I had spent the whole summer eating marshmallows with a hottie, I sure wouldn't be sad about it. You wanna trade places and visit Nana Kim in Scottsdale every year? All she wants to do is talk to me about my figure and grill me about why none of my boyfriends are Korean. And Arizona in the summer is *hot*.

> *Editor's Note: I know Nana Kim's retirement complex has a pool. So don't come crying to me, Coco.*

HUTCH: Avery had broken up with both Robby and Charlie, yet according to the evidence Coco provided, and Avery's own testimony, she seemed sad about it afterward. Why break up with them, then? What was this self-sabotaging instinct that drove Avery to end her relationships with no probable cause?

Editor's Note: I was almost regretting asking Hutch to help out. I mean, I wanted him to analyze the evidence, but I didn't like the way I felt—like I was just another protozoa under the lens of his microscope.

AVERY: Hutch's "theory" that I had any kind of self-sabotaging instinct was patently ridiculous. Sometimes boyfriends can be perfectly lovely people, but that doesn't mean they're the right person for you, you know? Hutch probably didn't understand this because he'd never had a girlfriend. At least, I didn't think he had.

HUTCH: Wait, what? AD, whether or not I've had a girlfriend has nothing to do with the project. We're talking about *you*. And Liam. Drop it, okay?

Editor's Note: I dropped it. But I knew I was right.

ALEX MANEVITZ, *final member of Hutch's Wizarding Warlord Association*: No, I don't think Hutch has ever had a girlfriend. Definitely not.

MICHAEL: Avery was the only girlfriend Liam's ever had. Maybe he decided to retire at the top of his game.

ALEX: He dated who? Avery Dennis? Sorry. Never heard of her.

> *Editor's Note: Patently untrue. You cannot be in a grade of sixty people and never have heard of one of them. He was being deliberately obtuse, and I did not appreciate it. Sources lie, Ms. Segerson! They lie!!*

MICHAEL: In order to understand the magnitude of this aberration, you need to understand the social order at San Anselmo Prep.

ALEX: Everyone in the popular group looks the same to me. It's just a large blond mass.

> *Editor's Note: Coco is not blond at all, so I don't know what this fool was talking about.*

MICHAEL: I know people like to think we're living in a new world order, where it's cool to be a nerd now, where dorks run the planet, where geeks are chic, etc., etc. But those people are wrong. It's cool to have a vintage Star Wars T-shirt, or to sport a Dothraki Flash Tattoo because you're *so* obsessed with a TV show even though you've never even read the original source material. But it's not cool to spend your weekends immersed in the world of tabletop RPG or waiting at a con for the TOVA auction to start. I'm sorry, but it's just not. It's cool to be a *casual* nerd. It's not cool to be the real thing. And me, Alex, Liam, and Hutch? We're the real thing.

HUTCH: Of course high schools have cliques. It's unrealistic to expect everyone to be friends. Every group just does their own thing, and that's just fine.

MICHAEL: The different groups at San Anselmo are so separate they might as well be different species. From an evolutionary perspective, why would a lion pay any attention to a beelzebufo?

Editor's Note: A beelzebufo is a prehistoric carnivorous frog.

HUTCH: No, there is no evolutionary link between lions and prehistoric frogs. AD, I'm slightly concerned about the data you're gathering.

LIAM: I'm not complaining about my friends, but those two weeks with Avery—it was nice. I hate to admit it, but it felt good to be part of that crew. God, that sounds sad.

ALEX: That's what they all want to think, isn't it? That we're all just *dying* to hang out with them? Believe me, I have no desire whatsoever to go to the next Tripp Gomez-Parker party. I imagine the conversation is *stimulating.*

HUTCH: Seriously, AD, it doesn't bother me. I really don't *care* who's popular and who isn't. I'm very happy with my place.

Editor's Note: I'd always just thought of my friends as my friends. It was weird to hear Michael and Alex and Liam and Hutch talk about us like we were . . . I don't know. It felt weird. I didn't like the feeling that Hutch has a place that's different from my place.

MICHAEL: I tell you all of this not because it holds any particular fascination for me, but because you need to understand the enormity of what Avery Dennis did when she asked Liam out in seventh grade. She upended the entire social order.

HUTCH: Avery asked Liam out, huh? My hypothesis was confirmed. Once again, we see Avery as aggressor.

AVERY: I politely reminded Hutch that two pieces of evidence does not a proven hypothesis make. Classic confirmation bias. It gets the best and the brightest.

HUTCH: Avery screamed, "SHUT UP!" and hit me with her notebook. I was starting to think we should go back to doing interviews over the phone. Or that I should have pretended the *Discover* interview took longer than it actually did.

AVERY: The bonus of the in-person interview was that Mrs. Padalecki put out a plate of cookies.

MRS. PADALECKI, *Liam's Mom*: Oatmeal scotchies. Got the recipe from one of those Nestle Very Best Baking books in the grocery store checkout line. Love that butterscotch flavor.

ALEX: *You're* Avery Dennis? Sure. Okay.

    Editor's Note: This guy is so full of it.

AVERY: I returned to school to start seventh grade single. But not for long.

LIAM: Something was different when I came back. I have no idea what it was. *I* wasn't any different. Oh, wait—I guess I got my braces off. But people who had never talked to me were saying hi. Girls were smiling at me. It was . . . confusing.

AVERY: It was the fatal combination of Liam Padalecki's summer tan and the braces coming off. Also, he happened to be having a good hair day. And I swear he was taller.

MICHAEL: It is impossible for a human adolescent to grow substantially over two months. Liam was absolutely not taller when he returned from summer break.

LIAM: When Avery Dennis—*Avery Dennis!*—sashayed over to my locker, I had no idea what was going to happen. How could I? I mean, if you'd bet me a million dollars, I probably would have guessed she had a question about the summer math packet. No, wait—we weren't in the same math class. Never mind. I had no idea what she was going to say. Not that I could form rational thoughts or coherent sentences around Avery Dennis. I just stared as she walked over, my mouth hanging open as my palms started sweating. I wiped them surreptitiously on my pants as she leaned against the locker next to mine.

AVERY: I panicked, okay? I snapped. I could not walk into that school single. I'd broken up with Robby because I thought I would meet a guy at camp, and I did, but now we'd broken up, and I was single *again*! It would have been way too embarrassing to crawl back into that school alone. What would Robby have thought? That I was a total loser, probably. To be perfectly honest, Liam Padalecki was the first male form I saw.

ALEX: Yes, Liam's locker in seventh grade was very close to the middle school entrance. I fail to see what this has to do with anything.

LIAM: She was chewing gum, which is completely forbidden. Which I know because I've gotten dinged for gum like six times, and Avery Dennis has never received a single consequence. And that's justice for you.

AVERY: I have no idea what I said. I guess I just asked him to be my boyfriend and walked away?

LIAM: She said, "Hey." I nodded. Remember—could not form coherent thoughts in presence of Avery Dennis. She said, "You're my boyfriend now." I nodded. She blew a bubble and walked away. It was so awesome. Like a scene from movie.

HUTCH: I'm sorry. I'm sorry I just—I can't stop laughing. Of *course* when AD asks somebody out, there's no actual asking involved.

MICHAEL: When Liam told me what had happened, I didn't believe him. Why would I have believed him? It was *impossible*.

ALEX: You're saying I was there for this? Sorry. I don't recall. Not all of us keep tabs on Avery Dennis's every move.

HUTCH: Listen, AD, Alex remembers. Liam talks about those two weeks a lot. *A lot.*

LIAM: Part of me thought I'd imagined it, honestly. Until I was making my way to my normal lunch seat, then Avery marched up to me and announced, "We sit over here." I followed her to the popular table, and there I sat, right next to Avery like I was Luke Murphy or something.

MICHAEL: My mouth was open so wide I think some chocolate milk dribbled out. I couldn't believe it. Could. Not. Believe it.

HUTCH: And according to the million times I've heard this story, Liam then proceeded to completely ignore Michael and Alex for the next two weeks.

LIAM: Yeah, I was a jerk, okay? Sue me! Who among us wouldn't have been the same, had they been in my situation? I was an awkward loser who was suddenly dating the most popular girl in seventh grade! This kind of stuff does not happen! It does not happen!

ALEX: Oh, Liam was in school for those two weeks of seventh grade he missed? I had thought he was in Space Camp or something.

Editor's Note: There is no such thing as mid-school-year Space Camp.

LIAM: I was a straight-up baller. I walked around school for the next two weeks like I owned the place. I put my arm around the back of Avery's chair when I sat next to her. Sometimes she'd let me hold her hand. And she even let me kiss her when she was sure no one was watching.

Editor's Note: When no one was watching? Forget Bizzy Stanhope. Maybe I'm the worst.

MICHAEL: Of course, what happened next was completely obvious. Hubris. The tragic hero's fatal flaw. Liam Padalecki flew too close to the sun.

ALEX: Did Michael try to get you to read his graphic novel? Don't do it. It reimagines Icarus from Greek mythology as a modern-day computer programmer. I created a page for it on Goodreads just so I could give it one star in a public forum.

LIAM: I invited her over after school, to study. Man, that was dumb. I ruined everything. In school I was keeping up a pretty decent facade, but I had put zero thought into what she'd see when she came to my house—because seventh graders are incapable of foresight, unfortunately. My mom let us hang out in my room because she's cool like that. Maybe if we'd stuck to the living room, I would have been okay.

MRS. PADALECKI: Yes, of course I remembered Avery. She's the only girl Liam's ever invited over. Very polite. All that pretty, long blond hair.

LIAM: And I just never thought about what Avery would see.

AVERY: There were, like . . . goblins . . . everywhere. His room was covered in tiny goblins.

LIAM: Goblins? I think she was probably talking about the Warhammer models I was in the middle of painting. But it doesn't matter what it was, exactly—the Warhammer models or the half-set-up D&D spread or the R2-D2 trash can. For Pete's sake, my room was practically wallpapered in Magic: The Gathering concept art. She was horrified. It was written all over her face.

AVERY: There were goblins everywhere, okay? I was scared! I had to get out of there. And I had to call Coco. I had to tell *someone* about the goblins.

LIAM: She whispered one word—"gross"—and walked out of the room. It was the worst moment of my life.

Editor's Note: I can't believe I said that. I was so mean. Nothing about this Liam Padalecki interview was making me feel good about myself.

MRS. PADALECKI: Oh, that's right—Avery had a stomach-ache, poor thing. Her mom came and picked her up. Whenever I asked Liam about her after that, he said she was busy with tennis.

LIAM: I wish she'd said something besides "gross." I wish she'd broken up with me right then and there. Or maybe she *had* broken up with me, and I just didn't understand. Because like an idiot, the next day in school, I walked over to sit next to her at lunch.

MICHAEL: It was like watching a car crash. I couldn't look away. Liam had been a supreme butthead for the past two weeks, but that kind of social humiliation isn't something I'd wish on my worst enemy, let alone the tiefling bard who sometimes contributes positively to our campaigns.

LIAM: "Can I help you?" She looked right at me and said that.
Editor's Note: I kind of hate myself.

HUTCH: According to how Liam tells the story, Avery looked like she'd never seen him before. Like those two weeks of surreptitious hand-holding had never happened. He knew it was over.

MICHAEL: The natural order was too strong. No one, not even Avery Dennis, could subvert it. Things returned to the way they always were. After all—a fish may love a bird, but where would they live?

> *Editor's Note: It was like this guy had never heard of a flying fish. Or a pelican.*

ROMAN HOLIDAY

AVERY: Leaving Liam Padalecki's house, I was feeling decidedly not super. If I'd learned anything from that interview, it was that I was a grade-A jerk. Maybe that's why I couldn't make a relationship work. Because I was a grade-A jerk.

HUTCH: I reminded AD that no one was at his or her best in middle school. Not even me. Once I made Ashley Jenkins cry in earth science because I pointed out that the mantle was labeled incorrectly on her diagram of Earth's geothermal layers.
  Editor's Note: Must ask Coco, Facebook stalker extraordinaire, to find this Ashley Jenkins person. It's rare that Hutch mentions a girl. Even if only in the context of making her cry over science.

AVERY: Anyone who was that invested in a geothermal diagram had bigger issues.

HUTCH: I'd rather be overly invested in a geothermal diagram than overly perturbed by Warhammer models.

AVERY: Talking to Hutch's friends had only made me feel *worse* about the Liam Padalecki situation. I had actually enjoyed myself at that interview, talking to them and eating oatmeal scotchies. They were funny! And Liam was such a nice guy—I can't believe I did him so wrong. For the first time, I started to understand why Hutch wanted to spend all of his weekends rolling dice with these guys in a basement. It was kind of sad that they weren't coming to prom, too. I hadn't spent a lot of time with them, obviously, but they were still part of our class. They should be there. And I definitely couldn't imagine the most important night of high school life without Hutch. But I knew there was no way I was getting Liam Padalecki or Hutch or any of them to go to prom. I wasn't going to mess up Ultimate Game Night by plucking all the tiefling bards off of his campaign and forcing them to dance.

HUTCH: I could not believe that AD had uttered the words *tiefling bard*. It had been a big afternoon.

AVERY: It was time to press on. But I could not deal with Sean Graney and his lack of neck on an empty stomach. So I kidnapped Hutch and started driving down the 101 to the In-N-Out in Mill Valley. There still isn't an In-N-Out in San Anselmo proper, despite my frequent letters to the mayor.

HUTCH: The minute I got in the car, the locks clicked into place ominously and AD literally said, "I'm kidnapping you." No, it was not the most relaxing sixteen-minute drive of my life.

AVERY: There are so many things I love about driving, but probably the best thing about being the person with the car is that you get to make all the decisions! You can force your friends to go everywhere you want to go!

HUTCH: AD did not tell me where she was going. She spent the whole ride screeching along with the radio and ignoring any questions I asked her, like "Where are we going?" and "Should I alert my parents to the fact that I've been abducted?" When we pulled up at In-N-Out, I guess I was relieved more than anything else. Where did I think we were going? I don't know, an abandoned warehouse where she would torture me by making me help her select the most flattering Instagram filters? Or decide which Facebook photos to untag?

AVERY: I ordered animal fries and a strawberry vanilla milk shake for me, and a double-double with lettuce, tomato, and onion for Hutch. Raw onion? Really, Hutch? When grilled onions are an easily accessible option? Honestly, it made me like him a little less.

HUTCH: It's like everyone woke up one day and decided to hate on raw onion. Raw onion has been a perfectly acceptable burger topping for eons. It adds *bite*.

Editor's Note: I think what he meant was "It bites." Because it does.

AVERY: I hadn't planned to kidnap Hutch for the entire evening. Especially since he wouldn't let me eat while I was driving. I was *hungry*, and those fries smelled good.

HUTCH: AD is already a marginally terrifying driver. I was not about to let her drive with only one animal-sauced greasy paw. I value my life.

Editor's Note: This is a total lie. I am an excellent driver. One time my dad cried when he was teaching me how to parallel park because I was so good he was moved to tears.

AVERY: But then, as we were driving by Creek Park, I saw a sign for an outdoor movie night in the park, and they just happened to be playing my favorite movie of all time. I could see the black-and-white shape of Audrey Hepburn from the street! So I parked in a safe and conscientious manner.

HUTCH: AD screeched to a halt, drove *in reverse* down the street, and then managed to somehow hit both of the cars she parallel parked between.

Editor's Note: There was no damage. Ergo, I did not hit the cars.

AVERY: I grabbed my food back from that fry hoarder and took a swig of my milk shake. Which is when I discovered that Hutch had never seen *Roman Holiday* before. How was that possible?!

HUTCH: Yeah, I know who Audrey Hepburn is. *Breakfast at Tiffany's*, right? No, uh, I haven't seen it. And that's all I've got.

AVERY: There was a gaping hole in Hutch's cinematic knowledge that had to be rectified *immediately*.

HUTCH: It's not that I have a thing against black-and-white movies. I just don't especially have a thing *for* them. My favorites? *Pacific Rim, Princess Bride,* and *Hook*. In that order.

> *Editor's Note: Actually a totally respectable list! Then again, it is inconceivable that anyone wouldn't like* Princess Bride. *Except maybe someone like Bizzy Stanhope, who has no soul. Bizzy Stanhope would probably love to marry Prince Humperdinck.*

AVERY: I grabbed a beach towel out of the mess of crap that lived in the back of my car and marched toward the screen, dragging Hutch along behind me. It was totally packed, but I found a space for our towel way in the back. Luckily, it had just started—Princess Anne hadn't even cut her hair yet. I spread out the towel and plopped down. With an inordinate amount of effort, Hutch folded up his long legs and sat down next to me.

HUTCH: I do not enjoy sitting on the floor. Who does? Well, AD does, apparently, 'cuz she plopped right down, crisscross applesauce, while I tried to find a position that was somewhat comfortable.

AVERY: I realized suddenly that Hutch and I had never hung out outside of school before. And that was *weird*. I'd seen him every school day for the past four years—I guess I hadn't realized I'd *only* ever seen him in school.

HUTCH: It was weird, hanging out with AD at night. It had been weird being in her car, weird stealing her fries, and it was weird sitting down to watch a movie with her.

AVERY: I felt weird around Hutch—something I'd never felt before. And not *bad* weird, just like . . . *weird* weird. So I sipped my milk shake, ate my fries, and watched the movie.

HUTCH: I was kind of surprised this was AD's favorite movie, honestly. It wasn't what I would have expected. What would I have guessed? I don't know. *Frozen?*

    Editor's Note: Frozen? *Really, Hutch?*

AVERY: In *Roman Holiday*, Audrey Hepburn is a princess who runs away from her royal tour and meets this beyond swoonworthy reporter while she's exploring Rome. They have amazing adventures together and she cuts her hair and they fall in love, and the end is kind of sad because they can't be together. She has to go back to her royal life. But I kind of like that it ends like that—it's real. And the important thing isn't that they're not together; the important thing is that they had this wonderful adventure together. And also that he didn't sell her out by publishing a newspaper story about her. That's important, too.

HUTCH: What did this mean, that AD's favorite movie was a love story in which love ended? Was she unconsciously following the model set by *Roman Holiday*, leaving all her Gregory Pecks standing alone in the Colosseum as she moved on to other adventures? Or was she drawn to the film because it reflected her own experience back to her? In summary: Did life imitate art, or did art imitate life?

Editor's Note: I had definitely had enough of these open-ended rhetorical questions about my psychological state.

AVERY: I guess I like it because . . . because I don't know, really. Maybe because there aren't a lot of love stories that show that you can love an experience, too. That you can love a day. That sometimes love is about finding out who *you* are, and doing things you never thought you could do. It's not always about the other person. Also, I love her haircut. Any movie with a makeover scene just slays me.

HUTCH: Did I like it? Yeah. Yeah, it was good. Really good. My favorite part? Huh. I can't, uh, remember, somehow. But I had a really good time.

AVERY: While we were watching the scene with Audrey Hepburn and Gregory Peck in the river, sitting close together on my old blanket that weirdly smells like Fritos, I realized that this moment, right this second, was an experience. And it was an experience I loved.

SEAN GRANEY

AVERY: This is not something I'm proud of.

BIZZY STANHOPE, *prom date of S. Graney*: Avery and Seany *barely* dated. It was way back in middle school, when relationships didn't even really count, and it lasted for all of two minutes. I don't think you could really even call Avery Sean's ex-girlfriend.

AVERY: I think it was some kind of reaction to Liam Padalecki. Maybe I needed a totally and completely opposite boyfriend— which Sean definitely was. He was like a reverse Liam.

HUTCH: I believe the phrase AD was looking for was "Negaverse Liam Padalecki."
Editor's Note: That is definitely not the phrase I was looking for.

AVERY: However, I do think it's important to note that back in eighth grade, Sean Graney definitely still had a neck.

HUTCH: AD said he had a neck? Sure he did. I'll believe in past Sean Graney's alleged neck when I see some photographic evidence.

SEAN GRANEY, *Avery's ex, Bizzy's current*: Yeah, Li'l Sean had some serious game back in middle school.

> *Editor's Note: If he referred to himself in the third person as Li'l Sean for the entire interview, this would be the shortest one yet.*

COCO: Sean is, um, sporty. Not exactly the, uh, intellectual type.

CRESSIDA SCHROBENHAUSER-CLONAN: Sean Graney is the stupidest person I've ever met. He makes Tripp Gomez-Parker look like a Turing Award recipient.

TRIPP GOMEZ-PARKER: Cressida thinks I could win an award? Dag, that's sweet. I always knew she had a thing for me. What? Who? Graney? He's an okay dude, I guess. He's a big dude. He was big, even in middle school. Like, who knew little middle school dudes could have muscles?

SEAN: Li'l Sean was mad ripped. Big Sean is ripped *and* big, but Li'l Sean was just mad ripped. His bigness wasn't there yet.

> *Editor's Note: I cannot believe I dated this moron. Was I suffering from a traumatic brain injury at the time? Liam Padalecki may have been kind of a nerd, but at least he was smart. And by all accounts, he'd been a good friend to Hutch, even if he was "a bit of a showboat on campaign." (Hutch's words, not mine.) Sean had nothing going for him*

except biceps. How could eighth-grade Avery have been that shallow? More horrifying thought . . . Was twelfth-grade Avery still that shallow?

BIZZY: Seany's dedication to his musculature has always been impressive.

CRESSIDA: Sean Graney is the textbook definition of all brawn and no brain.

HUTCH: Sean Graney and I don't have any classes together. But my locker is pretty close to Bizzy Stanhope's, and I have seen some things I dearly wish I could unsee.

SEAN: Things have always been easy with the ladies. They just throw themselves at me, you feel me?
Editor's Note: Please God tell me I did not throw myself at him.

BIZZY: Knowing Avery, I'm sure she just *threw* herself at Sean.

HUTCH: For AD's sake, I hoped she hadn't instigated this relationship . . . but all past signs pointed to the fact that she probably had.

SEAN: Avery Dennis? Yeah, we dated. I've dated every single hot girl in this school.

COCO: Yeah, I dated Sean Graney . . . once . . . for about a week . . . Shut up! This interview is about Avery, okay? Avery, not me!

SEAN: I saw her in the hallway and was like, "Whoa. You still dating that little weaselly dude?" She said she wasn't, so I asked her out. Boom. Li'l Sean had bagged another hottie. See? I told you Li'l Sean had mad game.

Editor's Note: I blame post-goblins-induced trauma.

HUTCH: Well, at least Sean asked *her* out, technically. Maybe that'll help AD sleep at night.

BIZZY: Let me remind you, again, it was eighth grade, and it lasted all of a hot minute. They. Barely. Even. Dated. No wonder Avery doesn't have a prom date. She can never hold on to a guy. This is exactly why she'll be going to prom alone. Which is probably for the best—she needs to get used to her inevitable forever alone status.

Editor's Note: The only bonus of counting Sean Graney among the exes: It was clearly pissing Bizzy off to no end. Mwahahahaha . . .

AVERY: This was obviously a dead end. I was trying to glean some self-knowledge from this horrible lapse in judgment, but if the fact that I'd dated Sean Graney was going to tell me something new about myself, I'm not sure it's something that I'd want to know. Maybe some things are better left unknown.

HUTCH: It seems pretty obvious to me. The most popular girl in school dated a football player. Even AD isn't impervious to clichés. They happen to the best of us. One time I bought a Star Wars Monopoly set just because it felt like it was something I was supposed to do. I don't even like Monopoly. Weak game play.

SEAN: How'd we break up? She ended it, man, she ended it. Didn't want to come watch me lift. I need a girl who can commit to a healthy lifestyle.

Editor's Note: Dumping Sean Graney? Probably the healthiest decision I ever made.

WAYLON UNDERWOOD

COCO: I like to call Waylon the "Fixer-Upper." Is it weird that I am an expert on all of Avery's boyfriends? I feel like it's weird.

Editor's Note: Not weird. I could draw you a pie chart of Coco's boyfriends broken down by zodiac sign. The Aries slice of the pie is disturbingly large.

HUTCH: There's no Waylon Underwood at our school. He must have left before ninth grade.

AVERY: Waylon had indeed left San Anselmo Prep after eighth grade. I wasn't too worried about finding him, even though we'd lost touch. But when I went to look up Waylon on my Facebook friend list . . . he had vanished. Gone. Poof. Had he unfriended me?!

COCO: Luckily for Avery, there is no Facebook-stalking challenge too great for the incomparable Coco Kim. Seriously. There is no connection too small. No profile pic too vague. If you are on Facebook, I *will* find you.

Editor's Note: Ashley Jenkins! I forgot to ask Coco to find Hutch's Ashley Jenkins on Facebook. I should start keeping a Facebook To-Stalk list.

HUTCH: Avery had told me many times that Coco could find anyone on Facebook, but I wasn't sure. Waylon Underwood had absolutely no digital footprint whatsoever. He appeared to have simply vanished.

COCO: This was the greatest challenge of my Facebook stalking skills to date. I won't bore you with the nitty-gritty—the hours of googling, the fruitless phone calls, the emergency M&M's snacking—but I found him. I told you. No man is safe from Coco Kim.

AVERY: When Coco finally tracked Waylon down, he was not where I expected him to be. Well, who really expects anyone to be living at an ashram in Arizona?

BIZZY STANHOPE, *still the worst, but unfortunately relevant to the topic at hand*: House of Light? Oh, yeah, I know that one. My mom goes there like twice a year to spiritually cleanse and lose ten pounds. It's, like, the best ashram outside of India.
    Editor's Note: Typical Bizzy. This is not an actual representation of what an ashram is.

AVERY: Waylon had renounced the world entirely. Did he really need to get away from me that badly? That couldn't have been good.

BIZZY: There are some people who live at the ashram full-time—I don't really get it. And then there are the normal people like my mom and a *ton* of A-list people in the industry who go there for short stays to recharge.

Editor's Note: By "the industry," she meant like celebrities and stuff. Only she said it in the most pretentious way possible. Obviously.

COCO: The House of Light *does* have a phone, but the people who *live* there aren't supposed to use it. It's for outsiders to call in and book their stays. I figured out where Waylon was, but I had no idea how Avery was going to get Waylon on the phone. I think the yogis who lived there were supposed to renounce technologies. Because of the energies or something.

BIZZY: The gift shop has these totally amaze Kabbalah bracelets. They're one of the reasons I have such good energy.

Editor's Note: I think her bracelets are defective.

AVERY: I did the only thing I could do. I called the House of Light and told them I was interested. But that I needed to talk to someone under twenty to get the youth experience.

HUTCH: Nothing about this was going to end well. I was waving my arms at AD, whisper-screaming, "STOP. PUT YOUR CREDIT CARD BACK IN YOUR PURSE," but she completely ignored me. Like usual. I probably should have tackled her.

AVERY: I may have put down a deposit on a weeklong stay at a yurt in August. Which was going to be problematic when Dad got the statement for my "emergencies only" credit card. Maybe I'd pretend it was a surprise for him?

PAUL DENNIS aka DAD, *father, partner at Dennis, Godfrey & Markham*: A yurt? Avery, why on God's green earth would I want to stay in a yurt? Is it adjacent to a squash court?

AVERY: There was no way Dad would believe the yurt was for him. But what else was I supposed to do? I needed to talk to Waylon!

HUTCH: She did what with a yurt?! AD cannot go to an ashram. She will ruin everyone's inner peace. Also, if Bizzy Stanhope's mom goes there, I don't even want to think about how much that yurt cost.
   Editor's Note: I don't want to think about it either.

COCO: I wondered if Waylon would be different now. Although the ashram was definitely my third-favorite part of *Eat, Pray, Love*. More eating and loving, please.

AVERY: It was definitely Waylon on the phone. I hadn't talked to him in forever, but I recognized his voice immediately. He *did* sound calmer.

WAYLON UNDERWOOD, *ex-boyfriend, on the path to total enlightenment:* It seems like a lifetime ago that my mom and I joined the House of Light. Well, perhaps it was—I suppose it was before I truly started living.

HUTCH: This House of Light thing is *serious.* I googled. Articles on *Huffpo,* a feature in *Goop,* celebrities wearing white linen pants, as far as the eye can see . . .

WAYLON: Yes, the House of Light has received its fair share of press over the years. Print, as a medium, can't really convey what the House of Light *does,* but I'm glad more people are hearing about it.

HUTCH: Is this a cult? Or a fitness retreat? I don't know, man; anything where adults electively wear uniforms gives me the heebie-jeebies.

Editor's Note: Totally normal reaction to the San Anselmo Prep dress code.

WAYLON: I've heard what people in the outside world sometimes call the House of Light, but it's not. It's a collective. Gwyneth understood.

BIZZY: Yeah, Gwyneth was totally there when my mom was there. They shared a yurt once.

Editor's Note: Sure.

HUTCH: It costs how much to stay there?! The only thing they're collecting at that "collective" is a fat stack of cash.

Editor's Note: I could definitely kiss that "for emergencies only" credit card good-bye.

WAYLON: My mom had gotten more and more into yoga after my dad left and credited it with helping her find herself. She wanted to move us to a place where her practice wasn't just part of her life, but was our lifestyle.

BIZZY: Would I *move* to the House of Light? Um, no. Those white linen robes would totally wash me out.

WAYLON: Did I want to go? Of course not. I told my mom she'd have to pry my Xbox out of my cold, dead hands. But I was only a kid, really—what else was I going to do? Find my dad? Tried to, and couldn't. So we left everything behind and moved to Arizona. I didn't want to go, but I'm so glad I did. Mom saved my life. Well, she gave me a new one. A better one. I was reborn in the House of Light.

COCO: I was totally fascinated that Waylon had completely reinvented himself, because this wasn't the first time. In eighth grade, he was completely reinvented by Avery. Some people are really susceptible to strong personalities.

WAYLON: Avery Dennis? Oh, yes, Avery with the long blond hair. Of course I remember her.

Editor's Note: Is this seriously my only distinguishing charac-
teristic? Why am I not more memorable? Had no one noted
my fine eyes? My elegant toes? My extraordinary attention to
detail? What about "Avery with the rapier-sharp wit?"

COCO: Waylon Underwood was a completely average boy. Average height, average build, pale skin, brown hair, brown eyes. There was really nothing memorable about him whatsoever— until Avery started dating him.

WAYLON: Up until eighth grade, I'd flown pretty much under the radar at San Anselmo Prep. I played video games with my friends on the weekend, hung out, nothing too exciting. Then Avery Dennis asked me out.

HUTCH: She asked *him* out? Aha! Another one to confirm my hypothesis! Oh, but I couldn't forget about Sean Graney. And Camp Kawawa Charlie, too. Shoot. Maybe that's AD's pattern—there is no pattern. Or maybe it was my weakness as a scientist, wanting so badly to see a pattern where there wasn't one that I created one anyway. Classic apophenia. What? Oh. Apophenia is the typical human tendency to perceive patterns in random information. We want to see connections so badly that our brain creates them even where no connections exist.

> *Editor's Note: Classic Hutch convo. Apophenia. Well, if*
> *nothing else, between this and the beelzebufo, I was learning*
> *a lot.*

WAYLON: Frankly, I have no idea *why* Avery Dennis asked me out—but she did, and everything changed.

HUTCH: This poor kid. Even over speakerphone, I could tell he was no match for AD.

AVERY: I asked him out because I thought he was cute, okay? And it's not like I made him do anything he didn't want to do! He just didn't have any *direction*. I was helping him! Motivating him! I mean, we were almost in high school. College was just around the corner! I knew he was going to need way more extracurriculars to eventually round out his college application. I was doing him a *favor*.

HUTCH: Who has direction in eighth grade?
  Editor's Note: Hutch is so full of it. In eighth grade, he won the Broadcom MASTERS competition and some LEGO thing sponsored by NASA that sounds dumb but I think is actually insanely prestigious. So don't talk to me about direction, Hutch.

COCO: No one even knew who Waylon Underwood *was*, and by the end of September, he was Student Council president.

WAYLON: Did I want to be on Student Council? No, no, definitely not. That was all Avery's idea. I didn't like talking in front of other people, or making decisions, or being in charge of anything. But Avery made it *sound* like a really good idea.

HUTCH: Why didn't AD just run for Student Council president herself? Disappointing. I thought she had more feminist drive than that. That she wouldn't want to just be the little woman standing behind the man in power.

> *Editor's Note: I didn't run for middle school Student Council president because I had already been Student Council president in sixth and seventh grade. Principal Patel instituted a ridiculous term-limit rule.*

PRINCIPAL PATEL, *principal of San Anselmo Prep*: The term-limit rule is necessary, and I certainly did not institute it solely to keep Avery Dennis out of a position of marginal authority.

> *Editor's Note: I do not take the following accusation lightly . . . but this is definitely a lie. The patriarchy was trying to keep me down!*

COCO: Oh, yeah, I remember the whole term-limit thing. Maybe Avery is more of an FDR than a JFK. I am not *nearly* as well versed in the Roosevelts, unfortunately.

WAYLON: Luckily, Avery was my vice president, so she pretty much did everything, but I still had to be in charge of the meetings. It was terrifying.

AVERY: I didn't know he was terrified! I thought he was having *fun.* I loved Student Council, so I thought he would love it, too!

...d be a nice way for us to spend time together

...y God, AD was the Lady Macbeth of middle school Stu... ...ouncil? I'm surprised everyone made it out alive.

AVERY: I was still busy with tennis after school, though, so I thought Waylon should probably play a sport, too, so we could train together. That sounds fun, right? At least, at the time, I thought it did.

WAYLON: I joined the football team when Avery suggested I take up a sport. I ended up being the kicker, and she'd come in and lecture the coach if she thought he wasn't putting me in enough. One time she offered him a giant basket of mini muffins in exchange for giving me more field time. He declined.

COACH OWENS, *football coach*: Yeah, I can tell you what our best seasons are. The seasons when Avery Dennis isn't dating any of my players.

WAYLON: Sports and Student Council weren't enough extra-curricular activities for Avery, though. So she assumed they weren't enough for *me*. But she said none of the existing clubs were prestigious enough, so she thought I would really enjoy it if I founded my own club, because she had had so much fun when she founded the debate team. My new club? It was a premed club—I think she called it Future Doctors of America when she filled out the new club approval form for me.

AVERY: When I asked him on our first date what his future career plans were, he had said he thought he might want to be a doctor! I know that med school is competitive—I was trying to give him an edge, that's all.

WAYLON: I said I wanted to be a doctor? I must have just picked something totally at random. I don't remember that at all.

HUTCH: This poor Waylon kid sounded exhausted just *remembering* the time he dated AD.

WAYLON: I didn't have time to play video games anymore. And I couldn't relax. I had no idea how Avery could do all of her activities. I was so tired, I'd fall asleep in my Cocoa Puffs every morning and nod off during fifth period. But Avery was superhuman. Who has that much energy? All I wanted to do was sit on the couch and eat cereal out of the box! Avery *never* just sat on the couch.

AVERY: I felt awful. I had no idea I'd caused Waylon so much stress! I thought he'd *liked* all the activities we did together. He was a good Student Council president, and Future Doctors of America was fun! And he looked so cute in his football uniform.

WAYLON: Mad at Avery? No, of course I'm not mad at her! I'm grateful to her, if anything. If I hadn't been so tired, maybe I would have fought my mom harder on the House of Light thing. I needed to let go of all these things that were dragging me down. I let go of all of them, I let go of the past, and now I'm light. I couldn't be the way Avery wanted me to be, but now I've found a way to just *be*.

HUTCH: Was there a lesson here? I think it was that AD needed to date someone who could keep up with her. There's no way a relationship would last with someone who couldn't handle her packed schedule. He'd hightail it out for the nearest ashram before the week was out.

Editor's Note: Waylon did not join that ashram because of me. He went with his mom. Also, he clearly loved it, so if it was because of me, I did him a favor.

WAYLON: Adherents to the House of Light can leave at any time—it's not a prison. But why would I want to go anywhere else? I was so happy that Avery was thinking of joining us here. I think it would do her a world of good.

AVERY: I'd forgotten about my yurt-booking slash little-white-lie-about-going-there. I told him to expect my dad in August, shouted, *"Namaste!"* and hung up.

HUTCH: It was a fittingly unenlightened end to the conversation.

ROMAN HOLIDAY, PART TWO

MARGAUX CLARK, *stylist/owner of Margaux Clark Salon*: You could say I've been cutting Avery's hair since before she was born. I remember when Pam was pregnant with her.

PAMELA DENNIS aka MOM, *mother, CFO of Brightstar Assets LTD*: I've been seeing Margaux for a cut and color every six weeks for . . . oh, I don't know, the past twenty years?

MARGAUX: I did Avery's very first haircut. All those little blond curls . . . so sweet! And I've done every one since. Oh, except for the time Avery's friend cut her bangs. Not her finest moment.

COCO: The bangs. Oh, the bangs. I'm sorry about the bangs, okay? It was a mistake! I know it was a mistake! I watched a YouTube video, and I thought I could do it!

MARGAUX: When Avery told me what she wanted me to do to her hair, I thought she was joking.

MOM: Avery's always been fussy about her hair. When she was fourteen, she destroyed all photographic evidence of our weekend trip to Big Sur because her hair was "doing a thing." An entire family vacation, expunged from the historical record. Forever.

MARGAUX: In the past, Avery had cried when I trimmed her hair. On more than one occasion. Anytime she thought I'd taken off more than an inch, cue the waterworks.

Editor's Note: Patently untrue. She was probably confused because my eyes are so sparkling.

AVERY: It was time for a change. Maybe the most depressing thing about interviewing my ex-boyfriends was the fact that the major thing they remembered about me was my long blond hair. How could my *hair* be my most memorable trait? The last thing I wanted to be remembered for was a collection of dead cells sprouting out of my head. More importantly, the Avery I had been wasn't the Avery I wanted to be anymore. The whole point of doing this oral history and my dating hiatus was to figure out who I really was—without a boyfriend and without an admittedly gorgeous head of long naturally blond hair. I was tired of being the girl who was never alone. And I didn't want to be the girl who had dumped Liam Padalecki just because he loved goblins.

MARGAUX: When Avery said, "I want this look to say, 'I am totally cool with goblins,'" I decided to ignore that and focus on the picture she'd provided.

AVERY: Maybe some of what Waylon said had stuck with me. About lightness. And letting go. I needed to let go and be lighter. Besides, I needed a new look for when I showed off my new self at the prom. I needed a haircut that said I was happy dancing on my own. Luckily, my lock screen background is a picture of Audrey Hepburn in *Roman Holiday*. So I showed Margaux exactly what I wanted, closed my eyes, and held my breath.

MARGAUX: I put her hair in a ponytail so we could send it to Locks of Love, and snipped. Almost two feet of hair. Gone. I kept cutting, shaping, and trimming Avery's hair, determined this was going to be the finest pixie cut of my career.

AVERY: I opened my eyes, and a stranger stared back at me from the mirror. I smiled at her.

HAIRCUT FALLOUT

NATALIE WAGNER, *random freshman*: This was the haircut heard 'round the world.

BECCA HORN, *random freshman*: I'm sorry, I will not comment on Avery Dennis's haircut. I will not comment on *anyone's* haircut. I have standards.

BIZZY STANHOPE: Avery looked like a boy. Like a twelve-year-old boy. And only days before prom! For the first time, I really believed in the power of *The Secret*. I had put it out into the universe, and it happened. Avery was ruined. No one was going to put a prom queen tiara on that freshly shorn head. She looked like Anne Hathaway in *Les Miz*. But with slightly better teeth.

CRESSIDA SCHROBENHAUSER-CLONAN: I couldn't imagine a less interesting topic of conversation than Avery Dennis's hair. And yet, it was all anyone could talk about. Incredibly annoying.

NATALIE: I swear to God, when Avery walked into school, it fell completely silent. Jaws dropped. People stared.

COCO: It was so brave. It was so *fierce!* She completely pulled it off. Her cheekbones looked amazing.

CRESSIDA: Did I *care* about Avery Dennis's haircut? Absolutely not. I had more important things to worry about—like trying to beat out Hutch for valedictorian. Everyone knows salutatorian is Latin for "not quite good enough."

HUTCH: It looked good. I think AD hides behind her hair sometimes . . . It was nice to see her face. Her whole face. All the time.

CRESSIDA: You should have seen the way Hutch looked at her when she walked into bio. It was . . . well. As I said before. Annoying.

> *Editor's Note: I don't know what she's talking about. Hutch barely looked at me and all he said was, "I hope you remembered your notes for the open-book quiz," so I pulled them out and waved them in his face. What kind of amateur does he think I am?*

COCO: One time I cut my hair shortish, like in a bob, and Nana Kim said, "Some of the worst mistakes in my life were haircuts." Which turned out to be a Jim Morrison quote. I kept my hair long after that.

NATALIE: Avery had this, like, wise smirk on her face the whole time, like she knew exactly what everyone was thinking. Like she had *made* them think it. My God, she's a genius. If I cut all my hair off, I'm completely sure no one would care.

BIZZY: Everyone knows men prefer long hair. It's in, like, every issue of *Cosmo* ever printed. Sometimes they even show pictures of celebrities and ask men which look they prefer, and it's long hair. Always. Every single time. Avery must have realized there was absolutely no way she could find a date for the prom. She did the smart thing and gave up. It was time for her to get some pleated pants and a subscription to *Cat Fancy* magazine.

> *Editor's Note: I already have a cat named Fromage, and he is a delight. And if Bizzy knew anything about cats, she would know that* Cat Fancy *rebranded itself as* Catster, *and all their good content is online. SO WHO NEEDS A SUBSCRIPTON ANYWAY, BIZZY?!*

HUTCH: What did I like *better*? You mean the short hair or the long hair? I don't know. AD was still AD. Hair is just hair. The short hair, I guess, if I had to pick? At least now you could see her face.

TRIPP GOMEZ-PARKER: Was she still hot? Good question. But actually, no question. There are certain kinds of hotness that cannot be dimmed. It would take a lot to make Avery Dennis un-hot. Like what? Um, I don't know. Rabies?

> *Editor's Note: Maybe Coco should go to the prom alone, too.*

NATALIE: It was absolutely and completely insane. Avery's hair was her *thing*. Her signature look. Her trademark. Like, who even *was* Avery Dennis without her long blond hair?

Editor's Note: That is exactly what I was hoping to find out.

BENVOLIO
SCHROBENHAUSER-CLONAN

AVERY: The haircut may have been my present, but it was time to dig deeper into the past and head back to another time of rebirth—ninth grade. One of the downfalls of going to a K–12 school is that you can't reinvent yourself as a hot new freshman. Although I'd basically crushed middle school, so why would I have wanted to reinvent myself anyway?

COCO: After we graduated from middle school, Waylon moved away, and Avery headed back to Camp Kawawa and straight into Charlie's tanned arms.

CAMP KAWAWA CHARLIE: The summer after eighth grade? I don't know, man, was that the year orange finally won the color war?
Editor's Note: This well had clearly run dry.

COCO: That summer was fun, but Avery and I could not have been more excited to start high school.

CRESSIDA SCHROBENHAUSER-CLONAN: Ninth grade was the year Avery Dennis ruined my life.

BIZZY STANHOPE: Mrs. Schrobenhauser-Clonan had volun-
.teered to host the ninth-grade back-to-school party, which was
ridiculous, because their pool is insanely small. Our pool could
be used to host Olympic qualifying trials, if necessary.

*Editor's Note: I'll be sure to let the Olympic Committee
know they can count on the Stanhopes in a time of need.*

CRESSIDA: I had so many issues with that party. First of all,
why does the school insist on mandating outside-of-school
forced social interactions? That's not normal. Secondly, a back-
to-school pool party? Come on. I should have asked Mom to
hand out souvenir tote bags with I'M PRIVILEGED printed on
them. Thirdly, why did we have to get to know each other?
We'd known most of each other for the better part of a decade!
I'm sure we could have gotten to know the handful of new
freshmen at school.

HUTCH: Oh, I remember that party. That was my first experience with my new classmates at San Anselmo Prep. What
about my old school? No, we definitely did not have back-to-
school pool parties there. I had no idea what to make of any of
this. After my mom dropped me off, I almost chased her down
the street, demanding to get back in the car and go back to our
old neighborhood and my old school. But I figured running
down the street after my mommy would be more embarrassing
than just going to the party, so I bit the bullet and rang the
doorbell. Cressida's mom showed me down to the basement. I
could see the pool and a swing set through the sliding glass

doors, but there was no way I was going out there. I stood in the corner, drinking a soda alone, until Liam noticed the twenty-sided die I'd turned into a key chain and hooked onto my backpack.

LIAM PADALECKI: Michael and I had been drinking sodas in the corner when I first saw Hutch drinking his soda in a *different* corner. You could say it was fate.

MICHAEL FEELEY: Alex didn't make it to the pool party—that evil genius faked a stomach illness. But at least I can say I was there for the day we met our once and future Dungeon Master. When Liam pointed out that key chain, I just *knew* we'd found someone special.
   Editor's Note: Maybe the real love story here isn't me and my exes, but Hutch and his wizarding dungeon friends.

LIAM: That was such a sweet key chain. Later, Hutch helped me make one the first time we hung out at my house. It's still on my backpack.

HUTCH: Man, I brought a backpack to a pool party. I was screwed from the start.
   Editor's Note: So weird that Hutch was drinking a soda alone in a corner of Cressida's basement, just like Robby Monroe. But seriously. Who brings a backpack to a pool party?

LIAM: No, I didn't go swimming. Have you ever seen me shirtless? I'm practically translucent. Seriously. I'm so pale I would glow under a black light. Swimming at a school pool party would be like sending Bizzy Stanhope an engraved invitation that said, "Please mock me." I would like to cling quietly to whatever shreds of dignity I have left.

MICHAEL: I don't own a bathing suit. Swimming is for chumps.

COCO: I was sooo happy. You know how much I'd loved Cressida's birthday parties! When my mom got the e-vite to the ninth-grade back-to-school pool party, the sadness I'd felt when the birthday parties ended was replaced by a beam of pure joy! Plus, I'd gotten a really cute new swimsuit and giant sunglasses. I had *just* discovered the magic that is Jackie O, and I started with the sunglasses.

CRESSIDA: I was so mad at my mom. I could make her stop throwing birthday parties, but there was nothing I could do when she decided to start volunteering for school activities. So I locked myself in my room and started rereading Discworld. Big mistake. Huge. What I *should* have done was watch Avery Dennis like a hawk. And possibly handcuffed her to the refreshment table.

HUTCH: Do I remember seeing Avery at the pool party? Sure. I didn't know who she was, but she was hard to miss. Really long, really blond hair, and a hot-pink bikini. Oh, no, wait—I can't believe I'd forgotten this—Liam pointed her out! "That's my ex," he'd said, shrugging nonchalantly. He mumbled some nonsense about how he'd ended things because he couldn't be tied down. I'd thought he was lying. And possibly crazy. But he was interested in tabletop RPG, so I figured he was my best shot at having someone to sit with in the cafeteria when school started.

LIAM: Yeah, people always think I'm lying when I tell them I dated Avery. I'm used to it.

Editor's Note: I couldn't stop thinking about all the times I'd shrieked with disgust when someone reminded me that I'd once been Liam Padalecki's girlfriend. And I couldn't even pin it all on middle school Avery. High school Avery had done her fair share of shrieking, too.

HUTCH: I guess we technically met for the first time a couple days later, when Avery sat next to me in bio. But I remembered seeing her at the pool party.

Editor's Note: I have zero memory of seeing Hutch at the pool party, which makes me feel bad.

COCO: The pool party ended up being even better than any of Cressida's birthday parties. You think Robby Monroe was drama? Please. I'll give you drama. This was the party where Avery met her older man.

CRESSIDA: I didn't think I needed to keep an eye on my brother. Why would I have needed to keep an eye on my brother? He was in his room, playing guitar. He'd expressed no interest in crashing a ninth-grade pool party. He was older than I was. He knew what he was doing. Or so I thought.

COCO: Avery was a naïve freshman. Ben was a worldly, experienced sophomore. I worried there was an insurmountable imbalance of power that would create an uneven relationship dynamic. A dramatic age difference like that can cause real problems.

AVERY: I reminded Coco that JFK was like twelve years older than Jackie O.

COCO: Whenever Avery dropped some all-too-convenient Kennedy knowledge on me, I felt confident she had just surreptitiously googled it on her phone to prove some stupid point. And also, as much as I love the Kennedys, that relationship was not without its fair share of problems.

Editor's Note: Of course I had just googled. What are smartphones for if not to win arguments against the people we love?

HUTCH: I didn't know Cressida had an older brother. I didn't even know Ben existed until he was waiting outside of bio to explore AD's tonsils every day after class.

BENVOLIO "BEN" SCHROBENHAUSER-CLONAN, *ex-boyfriend and rising sophomore at UC Santa Barbara*: Oh, sure, Avery Dennis and the hot-pink bikini. I remember. I was hiding in my room from all the kids in Cressie's class. Come to think of it, I'm sure Cressie was hiding in her room from all those kids, too. But I was a sophomore, man. I was sitting in my room, playing Phish on my guitar, very poorly. I thought I was so cool.

COCO: Avery had been talking about this party all summer. Well, writing me letters from Camp Kawawa all summer about this party. About what swimsuit she was going to wear, about how she was going to straighten her hair, although it's honestly naturally very straight, wondering if there would be any cute new boys . . . but then the big day *finally* arrived, and she vanished like two minutes into the party! Poof! Gone! Disappeared! I looked around for a bit, then gave up and went to put my feet in the pool. I was busy ignoring Tripp from behind my sunglasses.

TRIPP GOMEZ-PARKER: Coco was into me, man, she was so into me. Even back when we were little freshmen. But I made her wait for it.

COCO: Yeah, I know Tripp is . . . well. He's an acquired taste for sure.

Editor's Note: How I rue the day Coco acquired that taste.

AVERY: I was bored. No cute new boys had shown up yet. So I decided to go exploring.

CRESSIDA: That sneaking little snoop decided to just parade through my house like she owned the place. And then she stole the only thing that really mattered to me. What, Ben? No, not my brother! I don't care about him! I mean, I do, but, well— you know what I mean. Avery stole my one place of peace and quiet. My place of freedom. My escape from school. She invaded my *home*.

> *Editor's Note: Cressida should clearly have been in drama club.*

AVERY: I heard music. So I followed it.

BEN: I looked up, and there was this girl with long blond hair and a heart-shaped face in a pink bikini, leaning against my doorframe. I had no idea how long she'd been standing there.

AVERY: I'd been standing there for a while. But you know what they say: Time flies when you're watching a cute boy play guitar.

HUTCH: "They" don't say "Time flies when you're watching a cute boy play guitar." AD says it—more often than one might think it would be possible to fit into conversation—but "they" certainly don't say it.

BEN: I just stared. I was at a loss for words.

AVERY: He was seriously cute. I was aware of Ben Schrobenhauser-Clonan as an entity, as a sophomore at my school, as Cressida's brother, but I wasn't really *aware* of him until that moment. He was tan from the summer. His hair was a little long, curling at the back of his neck—he for sure needed a haircut, but it was cute. He was wearing a Che Guevara T-shirt, cargo shorts, and a hemp necklace, and I thought he was the coolest thing I'd ever seen. The guitar in his lap sure didn't hurt.

HUTCH: AD should have put on a T-shirt or something. This whole thing sounds indecent. Is this why we didn't have a back-to-school pool party in tenth grade?

AVERY: I was very decent. It was an extremely sporty bikini. I leaned against the doorframe and crossed my arms, trying with all my might to be as cool as I could possibly be.

BEN: She asked, "Does that song have any words?" I nodded. "Sing it," she commanded, and I obeyed. I should have started playing something romantic, but I couldn't think. So I just kept playing what I had been playing, which was "Farmhouse."

AVERY: The song was totally weird. It was about flies and stuff. But he had such a nice voice, and he could play guitar, and he was just, well . . . cool.

COCO: You know, I really consider myself lucky that the Ben Schrobenhauser-Clonan thing didn't kick off a Phish phase for Avery. The only thing I like about Phish is that ice cream. And it's not even my favorite flavor of Ben & Jerry's. I like Chocolate Therapy.

> *Editor's Note: Maybe I should have edited this thing a little more judiciously. You probably don't care about Coco's ice-cream preferences, Ms. Segerson.*

BEN: She said only one word—*good*—and walked out. I didn't see her for the rest of the afternoon. She was like my pool party Cinderella.

AVERY: I played it cool. For once in my life, I played it cool. It must have been my newfound maturity as a high schooler.

BEN: Well, I probably could have found her if I'd left my room. But I just kept playing the guitar. Also, Cressie had said not to come out.

COCO: Avery came back with a look in her eyes I hadn't seen since we made the enormous mistake of drinking all those Red Bull Total Zeros on Halloween in eighth grade. We ate all the candy that was supposed to be for trick-or-treaters, learned the choreography to *Thriller,* Swiffered my entire house, made homemade candy corn, dyed our hair with Kool-Aid, crocheted a blanket, and did all of my mom's Jillian Michaels fitness DVDs until we passed out sometime around 4:00 a.m. Maybe later. I think I saw the sun rise. But that might have been a hallucination.

Editor's Note: Please consume Red Bull responsibly. Also, don't give it to thirteen-year-olds.

AVERY: I saved Coco from the leering presence of Tripp Gomez-Parker—something I obviously failed at senior year, but at least I protected little baby freshman Coco—and told her everything about Ben and our magical meeting.

COCO: I was totally stunned. A sophomore?! Cressida Schrobenhauser-Clonan's *brother*?! But mostly I was stunned because Avery hadn't asked him out right then and there. No. She told me her plan was to *wait*. Avery. Wait. What kind of plan was that?

AVERY: It turned out to be a very crafty plan. And I didn't have to wait long.

CRESSIDA: God, how blind I was. What a naïve, Discworld-reading fool! When Ben asked me about the girl in my grade with the long blond hair, I didn't discern his true intentions. I know—it's embarrassing how obtuse I was. I realize in hindsight that it was incredibly obvious what his true intentions were. But I barely even looked up from my book at the dinner table as I mumbled the name Avery Dennis in between forkfuls of mashed potatoes. And with that fleeting admission, my whole world changed.

BEN: Even if Cressie hadn't known who she was, I would have found her. She was all I could think about. I started writing a song called "Heart-Shaped Face and Long Blond Hair." And another one called "Hot Pink Bikini." Oh, yeah, and "Pool Party Cinderella." They were all terrible.

Editor's Note: "Hot Pink Bikini" is actually pretty catchy. "Heart-Shaped Face and Long Blond Hair" has no redeeming qualities whatsoever. All I remember from "Pool Party Cinderella" was there was a lyric that went "Pool Party Cinderella without a flip-flop to her name," or something like that. I wonder if it's still on YouTube.

COCO: I thought Avery was nuts. She was heading into freshman year, completely single! This was a totally crucial time! Obviously, there is nothing wrong with being single. I had just never known Avery to *be* single. She always had a boyfriend. Or at least a plan for getting her next boyfriend. This time, her plan was just "to wait"? But she was absolutely, positively convinced that Ben was going to ask her out, and as usual, she was right.

Editor's Note: I think Coco meant "as always."

HUTCH: It wasn't long after I met Avery that she started going out with Ben. And the way they started going out was exactly as subtle as AD is. In that way, I guess, they were well matched.

CRESSIDA: Ben has done a lot of dumb things in his life—a lot—but the way he asked out Avery was hands-down the dumbest.

PRINCIPAL PATEL: Four years ago, playing musical instruments was not expressly prohibited in the halls of San Anselmo Prep. It hadn't occurred to me that was a rule that needed to be explicitly stated in the student handbook. Benvolio Schrobenhauser-Clonan proved me wrong.

CRESSIDA: I didn't think anything of it when Ben brought his guitar to school. Sometimes his band would use one of the practice rooms during a free period if they were available.

GEORGE LEURCK, *former member of the now-defunct band Grapenuts, current Starbucks barista*: Oh, man, when Schrobes asked me if I thought I could get a drum kit set up in the hall between second and third period, I thought, *Sick! School concert!* Then I found out it was about a girl, and well . . . Yeah, it was still pretty sick. Popped out of history early—grabbed my stomach and moaned, *"Emergency!"* and Ms. Segerson pointed me toward the door with mad expediency—met Schrobes in the jazz band room, borrowed the drum kit, and out we went to the hallway to set it all up. It was pretty sweet.

> *Editor's Note: I had totally forgotten that George called Ben "Schrobes." It sounds like a disease.*

PRINCIPAL PATEL: I suspected, at the time, that this guitar infraction had something to do with Avery Dennis. Addendums to the student handbook usually do.

> *Editor's Note: I took this as a tacit admission of guilt that Principal Patel had created his stupid term-limit rule to*

keep me out of power on the Student Council. I knew it. I KNEW IT.

GEORGE: I'd never seen Schrobes this worked up about a girl. I wouldn't have called him a grand-gesture kind of guy. He'd never asked me to get out the drum kit before, man. This was real.

CRESSIDA: When I walked out of science and saw my brother and that idiot drummer set up in the hallway, waiting, I assumed the drummer was to blame. Unfortunately, I was wrong.

HUTCH: I held the door and AD walked through. There was already a crowd gathering around the makeshift band in the hallway, wondering what was happening. But the minute AD stepped into the hall, it became pretty clear what was going on. The opening lyrics of that awful "Pool Party Cinderella" song included a pretty exacting physical description of her.

COCO: I can't believe I missed this. I was heading to my locker from Spanish on the complete opposite end of the building. It was the only time in my life I regretted learning the Spanish language. *Mucha tristeza!*

GEORGE: It was awesome, man. We were so jamming. I, like, legitimately believed the administration might let us keep playing the entire passing period because we sounded so good.

HUTCH: They were pretty awful. Or maybe it was just the song that was awful.

COCO: "Pool Party Cinderella! Hair so blond it's almost yellow! Lips as sweet as cherry Jell-O! Oh-a-whoa-whoa-whoa!"

CRESSIDA: I already had to listen to Ben's stupid band practice at our house every single weekend and alternate Thursdays. I did not need to hear them in the hallways of school. Yet as the first verse of "Pool Party Cinderella" recounted the story of Avery and Ben's first meeting, I realized my problems were far greater than my dumb brother embarrassing himself with his stupid music at school. No, this was no idle concert. He was *wooing* the loathsome Avery Dennis. And I was appalled. Because I knew someone as vapid as Avery would be completely taken in by mediocre guitar playing. Any monkey with opposable thumbs can play the guitar.

BEN: No, we weren't great, and it wasn't a great song, but I played with my whole heart. I sang into Avery's eyes and prayed she'd feel what I felt when I saw her leaning against my doorframe.

GEORGE: Schrobes was on fire, man. Don't let him tell you otherwise. That dude is way too modest. His vocals are always sweet, but they were especially sweet the morning of our epic hallway concert.

BEN: We got through about two and a half verses before Patel shut it down.

GEORGE: Dude, it was so rock and roll. Patel shouted, "Cease and desist!" so we stopped playing, but Avery—the Pool Party Cinderella, if you will—walked right up to Schrobes and planted one on him. Just threw her arms around his neck and started smooching. It was like something out of a movie.

CRESSIDA: I. Was. Appalled.

HUTCH: Definitely the weirdest first day of school I'd ever had.

AVERY: It was the most romantic thing anyone had ever done for me! How could I *not* kiss him? He'd written a song for me! And then *played* it for me! In school!

PRINCIPAL PATEL: It was utterly unacceptable. Obstruction of hallways. Disruption of classes. PDA. Total chaos.

GEORGE: Patel tried to nail me with in-school suspension for "misappropriation of jazz band materials," but since no jazz band materials had left school grounds, my mom argued him down to detention for "disruption of the educational process." Ben got the same thing. Also a lecture on PDA.

BEN: That detention was completely worth it. Because it got me Avery.

AVERY: Somehow I escaped with zero consequences and one smoking-hot sophomore boyfriend.

HUTCH: I'm not surprised AD didn't get in trouble. She's never gotten in trouble for anything. Including the time she brought a live pig to school.
Editor's Note: It was a very small pig. And she was very well behaved.

COCO: Like with many of Avery's relationships, she and Ben went from zero to sixty in fifteen minutes. The minute Ben got out of Principal Patel's office, they were inseparable. Walking to classes together, holding hands in the hallway, getting busted for making out by the lockers, all of it.

HUTCH: This school needs much more stringent policies on PDA. They were rarely, if ever, busted. I don't need to see that when I'm trying to learn.

COCO: They even sat together at lunch, bridging the freshman-sophomore lunch-table gap that was previously thought to be unbridgeable.

MEGHAN GOSSNER, *hottest girl in last year's senior class, current freshman Tri-Delt*: The nerve of that girl. Seriously. It was unbelievable. She just marched her tiny butt up to our table—*our table*, a table exclusively reserved for sophomores—and took the best seat by the window, right next to Ben. I fixed her with my most awful glare, which was normally so effective, but it didn't work at all. Avery Dennis was impervious to my death stare! I'd gotten rid of a long-term sub with that death stare! It was demoralizing, honestly.

COCO: Was I mad that Avery started sitting with the sophomores? No, of course not! She split her lunches between me and Ben. It was very equitable. You need to make time for your relationships. Like, Avery never got mad at me even when I made the huge mistake of volunteering to manage boys' varsity baseball so I could spend more time with Kevin junior year.

> *Editor's Note: It was a huge mistake. No amount of unlimited free sunflower seeds could make up for that time suck. But I never ever said, "I told you so," because that's what friends are for.*

AVERY: I was totally and completely obsessed with Ben. With all of my boyfriends, I'd mostly hung out with them at school or at camp, but that wasn't nearly enough Ben time.

CRESSIDA: She came over to our house after school almost every single day. This was before any of us could drive, so she would just *get in the car* with me and Mom and Ben. I sat in the front with Mom and cranked NPR as loud as I could. It didn't drown out the sound of their lovey-dovey cooing, unfortunately.

AVERY: We'd do our homework, sort of, but the best part of my day was listening to Ben play.

BEN: When Avery listened to me, I felt like a rock star. Mostly she'd just listen, but she'd hum along sometimes. Avery Dennis is a lot of things, and completely tone-deaf is one of them. Maybe that's why she thought I was so good.

HUTCH: Have I heard AD "sing"? Yes. Would I call it singing? No.

Editor's Note: I have never heard Hutch sing, so I tragically have no cause to mock him in return as he almost assuredly deserves to be mocked.

CRESSIDA: I hadn't thought it was possible, but Ben was now playing the guitar more than ever! I took to wearing my noise-canceling headphones around the house at all times. My headphones, however, couldn't help with the awful sights that accosted me. Avery Dennis, sitting with her stupid monkey-sock-clad feet up on my couch. Avery Dennis, wandering through the kitchen and eating her way through my cabinets. I didn't get to eat a single Annie's Cheddar Bunny for all of freshman year. She always got to them first.

Editor's Note: I am a sucker for a cheesy snack. Also, those monkey socks were adorable.

BEN: It was so great having Avery over all the time. She fit right in with my family. Mom and Dad loved her, and she got along great with Cressie.

CRESSIDA: She'd steal Ben's sweatshirts and take the best seat on the couch and hog the remote and make me watch all these awful reality shows and tell me everything that was wrong with my eyebrows. It was horrible. I was living on eggshells, terrified I'd do something she'd deem dorky and report it back to the rest of the popular-bots so they could shame me forever.
Editor's Note: I was honestly trying to help her with her eyebrows. I offered to pluck them and everything! I meant it nicely, like how I always do Coco's eyebrows. But I can see now why she might not have interpreted it in the best possible way.

COCO: Ben really only had one problem. A fatal flaw, if you will.

AVERY: His band practiced. A lot. And they played gigs. A lot. Well, I think you could call them gigs. They played at retirement homes, bowling alleys, teen centers, under a bridge, basically anywhere that would have them. And it was totally fine, at first! I loved watching Ben play. And hearing him sing. And the rest of Grapenuts wasn't half bad either. But that "at first" was key. That "at first" was where the problem lay.

BEN: Avery was the best. She'd come to every single practice and sing along in her off-key voice. She was always the loudest person cheering at all of our gigs—sometimes she was the only person cheering. Or the only person there. But if Avery was there, that was all that mattered. She was as loud as a stadium anyway. Yeah, she was the best. In the beginning, anyway.

AVERY: It's hard being a rock star's girlfriend. Who has time for all of that gigging? I had a social life of my own! It was so exciting at first, but then it just got exhausting. Plus, I was only a freshman, so I couldn't drive. Maybe the relationship would have lasted longer if I'd had a car.

PAMELA DENNIS aka MOM, *mother*: Oh, yes, I remember the Ben years. Year? It was less than a year? It felt longer than that. That was the fall I turned chauffeur. Well, into more of a chauffeur than usual. Sometimes Avery could get a ride with the band, but more often than not, it was the two of us driving up and down the 101. On the positive side, I think that was the only time I ever finished every selection for my book club. Those books on tape were a godsend.

> *Editor's Note: They absolutely were not a godsend. Nothing puts me to sleep faster than a book on tape. And then Mom would yell at me for not entertaining her. Hello, if you want me to provide scintillating conversation, don't put on a book on tape! You can't have it both ways, Pamela!*

COCO: Did I go to any of the Grapenuts shows? Sure, a couple. But they were just never-ending!

MOM: There are limits to what even the most indulgent of mothers can stand. About three months in, I quit. Avery would have to find her own way if she wanted to continue her career as Grapenuts's number one fan. And she did continue . . . for a while. For another three months, maybe?

AVERY: It was a lot, okay? It was too much.

HUTCH: So AD dumped him because of scheduling? Seems a little drastic. She could have just gone to fewer shows.

AVERY: At the time, it seemed easier to dump Ben than to tell him I wanted to stop going to all of his shows. I was afraid I would hurt his feelings! But now that just seems kind of . . . lame. And immature.

BEN: I didn't see it coming. Not at all. That girl ripped out my heart.

CRESSIDA: Of course I saw it coming. Avery Dennis is one of the most self-centered, immature people I know. There's no way someone like that can have a functional relationship with someone like Ben, who is, for all his faults, a kind and caring person. I'm only surprised she decided to cut off her access to unlimited Cheddar Bunnies. Maybe she'd moved on to a new snack food.

GEORGE: When Pool Party Cinderella dumped Schrobes, it kicked off a time I like to call Grapenuts' Blue Period. All of our songs were sad, man. So sad. There was "Broken Heart," "Heart Broken," "Endless Sadness," "Crying in the Cafeteria" . . . It was bleak.

BEN: I was a total angsty cliché. I can laugh about it now, but at the time, I thought my life was over. I would sit in class, openly weeping. What's really shocking is that no one made fun of me. An almost-six-foot-tall almost-sixteen-year-old just crying his emo little eyes out. Man, I never gave my classmates enough credit for their sensitivity.

CRESSIDA: Avery ruined Ben. He cried in school all day. He cried when Mom drove us home. He cried when we got home. He cried cuddling a tearstained picture of Avery. He cried playing those awful songs he'd written for her. He didn't do anything but cry.

GEORGE: I tried to break him out of the blues. I wrote a song called "The Cuttlefish's Backyard"—it was kind of like a tribute to "Octopus's Garden." I had always considered myself the Ringo of Grapenuts.

COCO: "If a cuttlefish invites you over, don't you dare refuse! There'll be a backyard swing set; we can swing in ones and twos!"

> Editor's Note: HOW DOES SHE KNOW THIS??? Seriously, HOW?!?! Guess I wasn't Grapenuts's biggest fan.

GEORGE: Schrobes was usually very receptive to my flirtations with songwriting, but not this time. Said he couldn't do the joie de vivre of the cuttlefish justice. He could only express pain through music.

CRESSIDA: I gave him some suggestions for song titles— "Avery Dennis Is So Not Worth It" was among my favorites— but he wouldn't hear it. He wouldn't even let me say anything bad about her! He just cried and cried . . . It was awful.

HUTCH: It just seems a little cold, dumping someone because you think he's overscheduled. Especially because he sounds like a, uh, extra-sensitive dude. That's all I'm saying.

COCO: I don't think she broke up with Ben because of his schedule. Or even because of Grapenuts. I think it was because of . . . the other thing.

> Editor's Note: Oh, no, not the other thing. I didn't even want to think about the other thing. I had hoped we could just talk about the schedule and move on. I guess that's what's so hard about recording history, right, Ms. Segerson? When

you *are your own unreliable source . . . It's hard to stay objective.*

HUTCH: The other thing? Oh, no. Usually when AD can't name what a thing actually is, it's bad. Like the Peanut Butter Popcorn Problem. The Nils Debacle. The Luke Murphy Incident. If this is just called the Other Thing, it must be *really* bad.

Editor's Note: I'm sorry, Ms. Segerson, but you'll lose all respect for me if I explain the Peanut Butter Popcorn Problem. I just can't.

AVERY: Nobody but Coco knows about the other thing. And Ben, of course. Poor Ben.

BEN: Do I remember what happened right before we broke up? Yeah, how could I forget? This was not a moment you *could* forget—much as I might have wanted to. I had never said "I love you" before. Well, to like, my mom and stuff, but never to a girl. But I had zero doubts! I was totally sure. We'd been together for about six months, and I was head over heels, one hundred percent, completely in love with Avery Dennis. And I couldn't wait to tell her. It was also, uh, Valentine's Day, so I figured it was perfect timing.

Editor's Note: The awful story was speeding at me like a train. Had I ruined Ben forever? This seemed like the kind of thing that could cause deep emotional scarring. Wounds that would never heal. Was Ben ever able to love again?!

I didn't want to hear this. But I knew I had to. And also I can't believe I destroyed him on Valentine's Day. WHO DOES THAT?? WHO IS THAT MEAN?! Me, that's who.

GEORGE: Schrobes told me what he was planning. I thought he was gonna want some drumming backup, considering I was there when it all began. But he said no. Wanted it to be private. Turned out to be a good thing, considering what happened.

COCO: Avery went over to Ben's house all the time after school. There wasn't anything out of the ordinary the day of, um, the other thing. Did I know it was coming? No. No, I had no idea. Ben and I didn't really talk much outside of Avery-related situations. Although . . . It was Valentine's Day. I guess I should have seen this coming.

AVERY: I had thought we were done with Valentine's Day. He'd left a red rose in my locker, which was totally romantic, and I was completely satisfied on the valentines front. Contrary to popular belief, I am not as demanding as one might think. Especially when it comes to gifts. I generally prefer the gifts I buy myself.

CRESSIDA: If I had known what Ben was planning, I would have stopped him. Instead, I sat in that car pool placidly listening to NPR, in complete ignorance of the total mortification that was awaiting my brother when we arrived at home.

AVERY: Ben went straight upstairs, but I went into the kitchen to get sodas and Cheddar Bunnies. We were allowed to hang out in his room as long as we kept the door open, and he had one of those squishy circle chairs that I totally love, so we did our homework in there a lot. I tried to make conversation with Cressida, but she was ignoring me, as usual. She wouldn't even look up from her book.

CRESSIDA: Blah, blah, blah. She went on and on, stuffing Cheddar Bunnies into her yammering maw. I was relieved when Ben called out for her and she took her sodas and snacks and got away from me so I could do my homework in peace. Had I gotten anything for Valentine's Day? No, no I hadn't. Well, my mom put a card in my backpack, but I don't think that counts . . . There was someone I thought might give me something, but now that I think about it, he's way too smart to buy into a holiday manufactured by the corporate greeting card conglomerate. Frankly, I think it shows far more regard for me that he *didn't* get me anything.

AVERY: All the lights were off in Ben's room, but he'd lit candles everywhere. Like a *crazy* amount of candles. He was standing in the middle of the room, guitar on the strap around his neck, smiling the special way he smiled whenever he saw me. I had no idea what was going on. He started playing a song, a new song, and the chorus was "I love you, Avery," and I knew I was *supposed* to feel happy, so happy, but I just . . . I just . . .

BEN: She panicked. Completely freaked out. I finished my song, said, "I love you, Avery," and she looked . . . horrified.

AVERY: I dropped the sodas. And I just *ran*.

BEN: Yeah, she just hightailed it out of there. Actually, I think she said, "I *can't*," before she dropped the sodas and started running.

CRESSIDA: I found Ben standing in the middle of his room, crying. I blew out all the candles before he burned the house down. Then I asked Mom if we could order a barbecue chicken pizza, because I honestly had no idea how to respond to this situation but figured getting Ben's favorite food couldn't hurt.

COCO: I found Avery wandering down Sir Francis Drake Boulevard. After I'd gotten a very distressed, extremely garbled series of texts, I came to find her. I got a ride from my cousin Dan, and then that turned out to be a whole different situation . . . but we can get into that later. I pulled Avery into Dan's car and buckled her seat belt for her. She was completely white.

HUTCH: But what I don't understand is why? Why had this happened? Aside from all the band stuff, it sounded like things were really good. What had gone wrong?

AVERY: *Nothing* had gone wrong. That was the problem. I just . . . didn't love him. And that almost felt like the worst thing of all.

BEN: No, I wasn't emotionally scarred forever. It sucked—it completely sucked—but that was, what, four years ago? Trust me, I've moved on. I don't even hate Valentine's Day anymore. The next time I told a girl I loved her, she said it back.

AVERY: I was horrible. No wonder Cressida hated me. I was exactly the self-centered person she thought I was. Only someone selfish would have run away from Ben like that. I should have at least, like, taken a moment to process, and started a dialogue with him, or something.

HUTCH: I thought AD was being a little hard on herself. She maybe could have handled things better, but she was only fifteen! I know the only thing I loved at fifteen was BattleBots.

BEN: Seriously, no hard feelings at all. Avery completely crushed me, but I think sometimes sixteen-year-olds need to be crushed. It builds character. It writes songs, you know what I mean? She was my first love and my first heartbreak. Grapenuts may have broken up, but my Pool Party Cinderella will always live on in my memories.

COCO: For someone who's had as many boyfriends as Avery has . . . has she ever been in love? Hmm. Good question. You know what? I don't think so.

Editor's Note: I don't think so either, Coco.

HUTCH: Do I think it's weird that AD's never been in love? Honestly? Not at all. AD's a pretty extraordinary person. It'd be hard to find someone who deserves her.

Editor's Note: Hutch was being bizarrely complimentary. All those watermelon Sour Patches I fed him to keep his energy up must have sweetened his disposition.

DANIEL KIM

COCO: This wasn't the first time Avery started a new relationship hot on the heels of the old one's demise. She's like a dating phoenix. Straight up from the ashes into the arms of someone new. When I asked Dan to help me find Avery after the Valentine's Day Massacre, I did not think I was acting as a new-boyfriend delivery service. But that's exactly what I was.

Editor's Note: Valentine's Day Massacre!? Really, Coco?!

DANIEL KIM, *Coco's cousin, rising MIT sophomore, ex-boyfriend*: I had just gotten my license. The only car I had access to was my mom's old minivan, and it was pretty horrifying. But that was the ride I was rocking when I met Avery.

COCO: Aunt May and Dan came to stay with us for a little bit, because my uncle had left them for his high school girlfriend. They had reconnected on Facebook and it was this huge scandal, because my family has, like, a very low rate of divorce compared to the national average. And also because I think people are always interested in social media affairs. So anyway, Aunt May and Dan had moved in with us a couple weeks after Christmas, but between school break and all the time Avery was spending with Ben, she hadn't met Dan yet. I should have seen this coming when I asked him to drive me—he is male, after all—but I didn't. I just saw a warm body with a driver's license.

DAN: It had been a very weird couple of months. But at the time, I wasn't exactly, uh, processing things. I decided to deal with my dad leaving us for some former cheerleader by ignoring it, bothering my dear cousin Coco, and focusing on my robotics team.

HUTCH: Robotics, huh? Coco had never mentioned she had a cousin who did robotics. I wonder if he was any good. Probably not. I'd never heard of him. I mean, not that I'm extremely well versed in current robotics competition stats, but I'm pretty familiar with the top tier of competitors. I stopped competing in middle school—there were other areas of the sciences I wanted to focus on—but I still liked to keep a hand in the robotics world.

Editor's Note: OMG, Hutch, jealous much?? The problem with this format, Ms. Segerson, is that it is impossible to convey tone. So let me just express to you clearly here that Hutch sounded mad jealous. Like how dare I know anyone else who is smart in science! Hutch doesn't have a monopoly on robots!

DAN: Coco was nuts on the drive over. "Containment is our chief goal, Daniel. We need to have a flexible response capability." It was like driving around with a very tiny, very chatty minister of foreign affairs.

COCO: Much of Kennedy's foreign policies can be proscribed to any kind of crisis. Rule one: Containment. Make sure the drama doesn't spread. Contain the issue to the issue itself. For example, your relationship has ended. That just means one relationship has ended. It doesn't mean you'll be alone forever. See? Containment works for communism *and* breakups. Rule two: Always have a flexible response capability. No two crises are alike. What worked for one breakup may not work for another. Be prepared to cry, be prepared to go to Taco Bell, be prepared to egg someone's house. Always respond to the situation in a flexible way.

DAN: After listening to Coco talk the whole drive over, the Avery I saw was not the Avery I was expecting. I was expecting a dynamo—maybe some yelling? Possibly angry crying? But what I saw was a sad, pale, quiet girl. Coco buckled her in and sat with her in the backseat, holding her hand. I don't think she said anything on the ride back to Aunt Alice's house.

Editor's Note: Aunt Alice is Coco's mom.

COCO: The afternoon of the Valentine's Day Massacre was a prime example of why the flexible response capability was so important. This was a brand-new breakup reaction. I had never seen Avery this quiet. Never. I took her home with me, wrapped her up in a blanket, sat her down at the kitchen table, and fed her some seolleongtang, which my mom had frozen and stockpiled in case of further Aunt May emotional crises. Wait—to be clear, Avery fed herself. I might baby my friends a little, but I don't baby them *that* much.

Editor's note: According to Wikipedia, "Seolleongtang is a Korean broth soup made from ox bones." Oh my God, I ate a bone soup?! Although actually, bone broth is really trending right now. I keep seeing all these models Insta-ing their bone broths. Coco has always been ahead of the curve.

AVERY: I was in shock, but I wasn't so out of it that I couldn't register that that soup was freakin' delicious. I ate three bowls.

DAN: The seolleongtang seemed to perk her up a lot. I'd also never seen anyone except my dad eat three bowls in one sitting, so I was pretty impressed. I was sitting at the other end of the kitchen table, tinkering with some mechanics. That was the year of the Rebound Rumble—we had to build a robot that could compete in a modified basketball game.

HUTCH: Oh, sure, the Rebound Rumble. I remember it only because it was an exceptionally weak year.

COCO: Dan didn't start coming to San Anselmo Prep with me. He went to Sir Francis Drake High—close enough that he could keep going there even when he moved in with us. And he could keep doing his robot team stuff. Oh my God, Dan's robotics team was the constant highlight of the Kim Family E-Newsletter. Headline after headline about his miraculous feats of robotics. And it's not just the newsletter, either. Seriously, every conversation with Nana Kim starts out "Oh, did you see how well Daniel is doing? That boy is so smart. Coco, you should be more like Daniel. Coco, what was the last contest you won? Coco, what is your GPA?" On and on and on about the robots he made and the awards he won and the perfection that is Daniel Kim. And when I made a pair of pants all by myself, did anyone care? No. No, they did not. Listen, I know it's not Dan's fault that everyone is obsessed with him, but that doesn't mean his brilliance is my favorite topic of conversation. Those pants I made had a button fly. Do you know how hard that is as a novice seamstress? And there was detailing on the pockets, too. But I knew Dan was going through a hard time, so I tried not to get annoyed by the robot parts all over the place.

HUTCH: So why are Liam's Warhammer figures unacceptable, but this kid's robots are totally okay? This makes no sense to me. What's the double standard here? Why are robots less embarrassing than Warhammer miniatures? I was also wondering if AD had some kind of secret nerd fetish.

DAN: I promise I was not thinking about making a move on Avery while she was sadly eating soup at Aunt Alice's kitchen table. I'm worried I'll come off like some kind of rebound relationship scavenger in this . . . What is this again? School project? Really? Huh. Okay. I noticed that Avery was pretty, sure—I mean, I have functioning optic nerves—but I wasn't about to hit on someone in emotional distress.

AVERY: I was in way too weird a mood to notice that Dan was cute. Well, maybe I noticed him a little bit. He has really shiny dark hair, and it kept flopping in his eyes in the cutest way as he worked. He has really nice hands, too. I couldn't stop watching him while he was building widgets or whatever. Oh, man, maybe I noticed him a lot. And on the same day of the Valentine's Mas—other thing! How could I have forgotten about Ben so fast?! Cold as ice, ninth-grade Avery. You were cold as ice.

COCO: At the time, I thought my mom had made some magic soup, but I think the real reason Avery started perking up was Dan. I had thought she was just staring off into space, but she was probably just staring at Dan. So she moved on fast. It's not a crime! Avery processes things more quickly than most people. Was I happy that Avery had moved on to my cousin? Well. Um.

> *Editor's Note: The following instances are probably the closest Coco and I have ever come to having an "issue" in our long and illustrious history of best-friendship.*

COCO: Listen—I love Avery, I really do. And in theory, did I have any problems with her dating Dan? No, of course not! Like, in an ideal world, I would love it if they got married. For sure. But it's a long way from high school to the altar. And Avery has a history of, a history of, well . . . I'm sorry, Avery. I don't know how to say this. I just didn't want Dan to get hurt.

AVERY: Coco never told me she didn't want me to date Dan. I just want to make that clear.

COCO: I didn't know Avery was going to date Dan until they were dating! It was very sneaky. I mean, I obviously wouldn't have forbidden it or anything. I just would have . . . Well, I don't know what I would have done. But I would have appreciated slightly more of a heads-up.

AVERY: There was no heads-up to be given. It was a total whirlwind romance.

DAN: She called it a whirlwind romance? I don't know if I'd go that far. Avery came home with Coco almost every day after school, and she kept migrating around the kitchen table, each day sitting just a little bit closer to me. Well, I found out later that's what she'd been doing. I didn't notice until she was sitting right next to me and her knee bumped my knee.

AVERY: Dan had a remarkable amount of focus for a teenage boy. All he saw were robot parts. I could have done a cartwheel through the kitchen and he wouldn't have noticed.

DAN: Yeah, I guess I'm a little, uh, obtuse when it comes to girls. And I was even worse back then.

AVERY: He was getting none of my hints. So I wrote, "Kiss me?" on a ripped-off piece of notebook paper and slid it right under his nose. *That* hint he got.

COCO: I went to the bathroom for two minutes. Seriously—two minutes! And when I came back, they were kissing. And that's how Avery's next boyfriend was born. Well, not born. You know what I mean.

BIZZY STANHOPE: Oh, yes, I remember Daniel, Avery's "outside-of-school" boyfriend. I'm using air quotes because it was totally obvious that Avery just made him up. Avery mysteriously gets a boyfriend none of us have ever seen before, who just happens to be her best friend's cousin? Please. It's too convenient. Daniel Kim never existed. Avery created a pretend boyfriend because she obviously went insane when she dumped Ben Schrobenhauser-Clonan and her mind couldn't deal with the trauma of being single.

HUTCH: I was always happier when AD was dating someone outside of school. Meant I didn't have to watch her make out with whoever the boyfriend of the moment was.

Editor's Note: Who knew Hutch was such a puritan about PDA? He could have a promising career as a high school dance chaperone. Maybe here at San Anselmo Prep. Our chaperones are tough. One time, Bizzy Stanhope got busted for inappropriate dancing and it was amazing.

COCO: I wanted to be happy for them—I really, really did—but it was just awkward! My best friend and my cousin. My cousin and my best friend! And every time I turned a corner, there they were, kissing. Nowhere was safe!

Editor's Note: Did I just spend all of freshman year terrorizing people by making out with their male relatives in their homes? Because that's kind of what it sounds like. I'm sorry, Coco!

DAN: I feel like I wasn't as sensitive as I could have been—Coco ended up being a major third wheel. I probably should have taken Avery *out* of the house more. But I was sixteen and stupid. I thought Avery watching me make robots was a perfect relationship.

AVERY: It wasn't as boring as it sounds, honestly. It wasn't thrilling, but it wasn't awful. We really didn't leave Coco's house that much, though. I think we went to the movies once? God, no wonder Bizzy Stanhope thought Dan was imaginary.

HUTCH: The art of robotics construction can be fascinating—in the right hands. But it's hard to imagine anything approaching artistry coming from someone who participated in the Rebound Rumble.

COCO: I wasn't jealous or anything. I just missed having Avery and me time—*just* Avery and me.

AVERY: And I missed having Coco and me time. It was weird how dating someone who had literally brought me closer—geographically, I mean—to Coco than ever made me feel more far away from her than ever! I didn't like forcing my best friend to constantly third-wheel. Maybe this could have worked out if Coco had a boyfriend who also lived in her house, but that seems like an uncomfortable situation at best, and a sister-wives situation at worst. I probably would have broken up with Dan eventually because it was weird dating someone who lived with Coco, or because I got tired of watching him build robots, but something bigger intervened. Something bigger than me or Dan or Coco or any of us. Something as big as . . . a whole country.

DAN: We had a good thing going, for sure. But I couldn't compete with Italy. Who could?

FABRIZIO MONTEFIORE

AVERY: I was going to the *nazione d'amore*. And I knew I had to go there single.

COCO: The minute I heard that Avery was going to Italy, I *knew* Dan was toast. As if Avery would pass up a chance to date some cute Italian boy! No way. Not possible. Dan didn't seem too upset by the breakup, though. Maybe his robots had taught him how not to feel.

DAN KIM: Did Coco make another robots-don't-have-feelings joke? I can *feel*. I just wasn't particularly upset about Avery breaking up with me. Things were getting really busy with competition season anyway, and it made more sense to be single. Easier to focus.

Editor's Note: Obviously, I'm glad that I didn't cause Dan any undue emotional distress, but his complete lack of emotional distress was slightly unflattering.

HUTCH: I hoped that last interview hadn't been too hard for AD. She must have been so embarrassed that one of her exes had been crushed so thoroughly by the University of Maryland at this year's RASC-AL Robo-Ops competition. From what I gathered from the robotics blogosphere, it was pretty brutal.

COCO: Back in freshman year, it was *arrivederci*, Dan, and ciao, Fabrizio. Avery took her dating game international.

AVERY: My dad wouldn't let me go back to Camp Kawawa after freshman year—he said it was time for me to spend more "productive" summers so my college applications would look better. But I found something that was even better than Camp Kawawa and Charlie's s'mores-scented embrace. I found a way to get to Europe *without* my parents.

ANNABETH NESS, *Director of Teen Travel Trip Programming, European Division*: All students on Teen Travel Trips are fully supervised one hundred percent of the time. That is a personal guarantee I make to parents and guardians.

AVERY: Sure, Teen Travel Trips *looked* educational—from the brochures. It definitely looked educational enough to get Dad on board. And I would absolutely conjugate some verbs if I had to. But grammar was the last thing on my mind. I was heading over to Italy with only three things in mind: gelato, amore, and fulfilling my lifelong dream of riding on the back of a Vespa.

ANNABETH: I may not *personally* accompany the students on any of our trips, but I am one hundred percent confident that all Teen Travel Trip counselors, chaperones, and staff uphold the high standards that I have set for all Teen Travel Trip employees.

AVERY: The supervision on my Teen Travel Trip was lax at best. There were forty high school kids and four counselors in their early twenties. Frankly, I think the counselors were worse than we were.

COCO: No, I didn't get to go to Italy with Avery. My mom thinks Italy is full of butt pinchers and pickpockets. So that summer, I started volunteering at the Moya del Pino reference library in the hopes that next year, my mom would let me apply to an internship at the JFK Presidential Library in Boston. It was a very quiet, very dusty summer.

Editor's Note: Spoiler alert—Coco got that internship and she's gone back every summer since. She revolutionized that boring old library's social media platform, and the entire staff of the JFK Presidential Library is completely obsessed with her. If you ask me, JFK's biggest flaw was being from Massachusetts, because Coco is going to college in stupid Boston so she can keep archiving with those dumb presidential librarians. Why couldn't Coco have been obsessed with Ronald Reagan? His presidential library is only thirty-four minutes from Pepperdine! But Coco fell asleep when I showed her Reagan: American Experience on PBS, so that wasn't happening. Curse you, Gipper!

HUTCH: I cannot believe AD's parents let her go to Italy alone. I also can't believe there wasn't some kind of international incident.

AVERY: I've always felt that I had a bit of European flair about me, so Italy seemed like my destiny. I stuffed my suitcase full of chic tiny neck scarves and jetted off to Rome.

HUTCH: Tiny neck scarves! *Roman Holiday!* It's all coming full circle now. I was wondering why she went to Italy when San Anselmo Prep doesn't even offer Italian.

AVERY: But because I am a born-and-raised Californian, I couldn't spend the whole summer away from the beach. So I picked the trip that would give me a couple days in Rome and then the rest of the summer would be on the beach in Riomaggiore, where I could wear Audrey Hepburn–style tiny neck scarves with my bikini. Best of both worlds.

HUTCH: San Anselmo is forty-five minutes from the beach. We're not all wandering around with surfboards, despite what Avery might have you think.
    Editor's Note: It's called having pride in your state, Hutch! California has the best beaches in the world. Also, just because I can't go to the beach as much as I'd like doesn't

mean I don't love it. And forty-five minutes is a nothing drive. Hutch hates the feeling of sand between his toes, so his opinion on the beach is irrelevant. He once called sand "nature's glitter," and he didn't mean it as a compliment. Although he does have a point about it getting everywhere and being impossible to clean up . . .

JANELLE DEMARIA, *senior at Short Hills High School, Avery's Teen Travel Trip roommate*: I knew Avery and I were going to get along from the very first day I met her. We had to go around in a circle and say what we were most excited about in Italy, and Avery said she wanted to ride on the back of a Vespa. You ever see *When in Rome?* With Mary-Kate and Ashley? That movie's crazy old but still awesome, in a so-bad-it's-awesome way. When I met Avery, I felt like I had found the Mary-Kate to my Ashley.

AVERY: Rome was . . . not exactly what I expected. This wasn't the Rome of Audrey Hepburn.

JANELLE: I feel like nobody wants to say anything bad about Italy, because who gets salty about a European vacation, but whatever, I'll say it. It was crazy hot. And super crowded. Why didn't Mary-Kate and Ashley sweat, huh? I spent all of Rome unsuccessfully trying not to sweat my eyeliner off.

AVERY: But there was something worse than the heat and the crowds and the dirt and the noise. Where were all the cute boys? I hadn't seen a single Vespa I wanted to ride on. I was starting to panic.

JANELLE: I told Avery not to worry. My sister had done a Teen Travel Trip two years ago and met *the* hottest guy in Cinque Terre. That's why I signed up for the trip that went to Riomaggiore. I figured there must be something in the water there.

> *Editor's Note: Cinque Terre is a region on the west coast of Italy made up of five towns. Riomaggiore is the southernmost town. They are all super beautiful but IMHO, Riomaggiore is the most beautiful of all.*

FABRIZIO MONTEFIORE, *ex-boyfriend*: I saw Avery the first day she arrived in Riomaggiore. I saw her right away. I knew she was a real American girl—real California girl. She was like from a movie.

> *Editor's Note: OMG I forgot how much I loooooved listening to Fabrizio talk. Who knew "Avery" could sound like "Aaavaarrrreeee"?*

AVERY: We got off the bus in Riomaggiore—of course I had total bus hair, ugh—and it was like stepping into a fairy tale.

HUTCH: Oh good lord, AD and the "bus hair." Every time we go on a school trip, she's convinced her hair has undergone some sort of chemical process that transforms it into the dreaded "bus hair." It looks exactly the same when she gets off the bus as it did when she got on the bus. Hey, maybe now that Avery has short hair, bus hair won't be part of our lives anymore!

Editor's Note: If anything, this short haircut is only going to make my bus hair worse! But I just realized that I probably won't be on a bus with Hutch again anytime soon. We definitely won't be going on field trips together anymore. Huh. That's kind of sad. Who knew I could be nostalgic for bus hair?

AVERY: If you've never seen a picture of Riomaggiore, I strongly suggest you google image search it right now. There are all these brightly colored houses built into the hillside, right above water so blue it looks like the Caribbean. Riomaggiore is basically a tropical vacation destination but with better-quality carbs.

FABRIZIO: My family has run *una pensione*—a small hotel—in Riomaggiore for generations. My father began hosting Teen Travel Trips fifteen years ago, so I have seen many American girls come through our hotel. But I had never seen one like Avery.

HUTCH: Wait a minute. Hold up. This guy had a new group of young, dumb teenagers coming through his family's hotel every summer? He must have been a huge player.

Editor's Note: When his family started hosting Teen Travel Trips, Fabrizio was four. I think the teenage girls were safe, Hutch.

FABRIZIO: I was running late. Mama had warned me to be there to meet the bus, but the Americans were already *off* the bus when I pulled up in front of our hotel. I knew Mama would be angry!

AVERY: It was a miracle. A young Gregory Peck drove up on a Vespa and stopped right in front of our hotel. He was even wearing a suit. A suit!

FABRIZIO: Yes, Mama always makes me wear a suit to greet the Americans. I do not mind it, so much. A nice suit, it is an important thing. The Americans, they did not dress so well, not usually. Avery, she was different.

AVERY: When I met Fabrizio, I was wearing a short-sleeved white button-down shirt tucked into a full navy blue circle skirt and of course a little striped neck scarf. I went the full Audrey. Ordinarily, I would wear sweatpants on a bus, but I didn't bring a single pair of sweatpants to Italy. That seemed like the kind of garment they might seize at customs for being horribly un-chic. I even brought a full-on pajama suit to sleep in.

JANELLE: When Fabrizio rode into the piazza in front of the hotel, Avery was squeezing my arm so hard I thought she was gonna leave nail marks. Was I surprised when I saw him? No way. I knew the magic of Cinque Terre would deliver. Like an idiot, I'd gone and gotten myself involved with another kid on our trip who was from exotic Maplewood. Why hadn't I held out?? Avery would have to live the Italian dream for both of us.

ANNABETH: Romantic relationships between fellow Teen Travel Trip students are strictly prohibited, as are relations of any nature between Teen Travel Trip students and young people who are not affiliated with the program.

FABRIZIO: Of course I had been in love before. A hundred times. A thousand! But every love is different. And Avery, she was special.

HUTCH: Man, this guy was like a cliché of a cliché.

FABRIZIO: I pressed my hand to my heart and staggered, struck by the force of her beauty. She giggled with her friend, the pretty one with the dark hair, and from that moment Avery, she had my heart.

HUTCH: I wouldn't be surprised if it turned out Fabrizio had fed the same line to AD's roommate, too. I didn't like the way he was talking about her. There was something definitely fishy about this guy.

JANELLE: No way. Fabrizio never hit on me! He was so into Avery it was ridiculous. I was definitely the Nurse and not the Rosaline in this situation.

Editor's Note: Nice literary ref, Janelle.

FABRIZIO: I blew Avery a kiss, and then Mama shooed me inside to help Papa with the keys. But I could tell by the dancing in Avery's eyes that her heart had caught my kiss.

Editor's Note: At "dancing in Avery's eyes," Hutch pretended to barf into my trash can. All science and no poetry, that Hutch.

JANELLE: The minute Avery and I got into our room, we started talking about the mystery guy on the Vespa. And then we pretty much talked about him the rest of the night, even as we plowed our way through huge bowls of trenette with pesto, which must have been attractive.

AVERY: I didn't see him again for the rest of the night, until Janelle and I were getting into bed, when I heard something hit our window. Then another something. Fabrizio was legit throwing pebbles at our window, like in a movie! Janelle and I raced to the window, and I was so grateful for my adorable striped pajama suit.

JANELLE: I was wearing this horrible tank top that said TASTEE on it. But whatever, it wasn't about me. Fabrizio called out, *"Mia cara bionda ragazza!* I burn for you! I yearn for you! I die for you!" A couple stray cats yowled, but it was still completely romantic.

HUTCH: I'm sorry—seriously? Are people seriously buying this? This is the cheesiest, most ridiculous, insane thing I've ever heard of! Who would be into this? The whole thing reeks of phoniness.

Editor's Note: It's called a grand gesture, Hutch! It was like he'd never seen a romantic comedy.

155

FABRIZIO: I told Avery everything in my heart until Mama found me and told me I was disturbing the neighbors so I must come inside.

AVERY: I think it speaks to the level of supervision at Teen Travel Trips that it was Fabrizio's *mom* who came and got him, not any of our alleged chaperones.

HUTCH: This whole thing sounds completely unacceptable. One benefit of AD swearing off dating is that she'd now be far away from guys like *this*. I think I'll be leaving a very strongly worded review on Teen Travel Trips' Yelp page.

JANELLE: I didn't even think they'd made plans to meet, but when we got out of class the next day for free time, there Fabrizio was, waiting on his Vespa. It was like they could communicate without words.

AVERY: I wouldn't call myself *fluent* in Italian, per se, but I would go so far as to say I'm remarkably proficient. Brilliantly proficient, maybe.

FABRIZIO: Avery's Italian, it is not so good. But we spoke the language of love. And also my English, it is very excellent.

AVERY: Listen to me *parlo Italiano. Fior di Latte, Cioccolate, Limone, Zuppa Inglese, Bacio, Frutti di Bosco, Nocciola* . . .

FABRIZIO: She can order many, many kinds of gelato. But these are her limits.

> *Editor's Note: Limits? Please! La Dolce Vita, La Vita e Bella . . . hmm. Well, sue me. I was out of practice.*

AVERY: After class on our first full day in Riomaggiore, I took the helmet Fabrizio offered me—because safety is even more important than hair—and climbed on the back of his Vespa like it was my destiny. *Which it was.*

JANELLE: Avery just hopped right up on that Vespa and they drove away. Nobody even tried to stop her! I guess the chaperones weren't paying attention. I looked at Brian from Maplewood and regretted all of my life choices.

AVERY: First we drove to a bakery and Fabrizio bought me a warm bag of what turned out to be the best focaccia I'd ever had in my entire life. Then he drove to the beach, and we sat on the rocks and ate focaccia and watched the waves roll in, and when he kissed me, I felt like I was in a movie. *Riomaggiore Holiday.*

FABRIZIO: *Un bacio perfetto.*

HUTCH: Let the record show that this clown made a horrible kissing noise that was audible over a transcontinental phone connection, like a cartoon chef presenting a plate of tortellini.

AVERY: Let the record show that *I* determine the historical record, not one James "Hutch" Hutcherson.

HUTCH: I was just trying to keep AD objective! All dealings with this Montefiore character clearly needed a healthy dose of skepticism.

FABRIZIO: My Avery, she gave me the most magical summer of my young life.

AVERY: Honestly? I can't really think of any other way to describe it. *Molto magico!*

HUTCH: Magical? Let's all take it down a notch, here. So he can wear a suit and buy bread and drive a dumb tiny scooter. But who *is* this guy? All I'm hearing is he does this and he does that—all about the things he does, but nothing about who he *is*. Did you guys ever even have a conversation?

AVERY: Fabrizio and I absolutely had conversations! But some-how . . . I couldn't remember anything about any of them.

FABRIZIO: I told Avery I loved her every day, every night, every hour! But she could never say it back. *La mia principessa di ghiaccio.*

> *Editor's Note: Oh, right. That's what we talked about. Well, that's what Fabrizio talked about.*

HUTCH: Avery cannot have been into that. For someone who dates as much as she does, she's usually not the mushy, saccharine type. That's one of the things I like best about her.

Editor's Note: !!!! A compliment, from the great James Hutcherson?!

COCO: Wow—the dramatic juxtaposition that was Avery's freshman year just occurred to me. First, Ben said he loved her, and that was too much. So she started dating Dan, who, I am one hundred percent confident, did not profess his love, since the only thing Dan loves is robots. Then she left robot boy and started dating the florid Fabrizio! Wait—maybe *florid* was not the right word choice. But what I *meant* was that she went from lovey-dovey Ben to stone-cold Dan to mucho-amore Fabrizio, looking for the right fit, yet none of it was right! She was like the Goldilocks of love.

Editor's Note: "Mucho amore" is not Italian. And aren't we all Goldilockses of love, searching for the right fit?

HUTCH: I don't think we even need to get into this breakup. Seems pretty obvious to me: Avery dates her idea of an Italian boy cliché, Fabrizio dates his idea of a California girl cliché, they spend a "magical" summer together straight out of a Disney Channel original movie, then Avery dumps him and comes back home to America. How'd I do?

Editor's Note: It was like Hutch had been right there on the shores of Riomaggiore with us.

FABRIZIO: As our beautiful summer drew to a close, I told Avery my love could cross an ocean! *Non c'e problema!* But no, she would not hear of it. "Long distance is the wrong distance," she told me. This phrase, I had not heard it before. But it was sharp as daggers on my ears.

HUTCH: I was ready to wrap this up. This guy's voice was like "daggers on my ears."

FABRIZIO: I cried many, many tears. I did love again, of course! *Ma certamente!* But no one was like my Avery. How do I feel? I am not bitter toward her! Never! I love always our memories of our wonderful summer. If only I could see her again! But she lives on happily, forever in my heart. *Che peccato.*

HUTCH: *Che peccato?* Please. It was time to wrap this non-sense up. We had learned absolutely nothing, except that foreign accents make even normally rational, stable girls lose their minds.

> *Editor's Note: I think we also learned that Hutch has a bizarre vendetta against Vespa-life. That boy doesn't deserve to eat pizza. Moving on.*

PROM COMMITTEE, PART TWO

AVERY: There is nothing worse than when real life intervenes in the middle of your extremely important research project—which is also, let's not forget, a school assignment and a requirement for graduation. But when I became head of the Prom Committee, that was not a responsibility I undertook lightly. It was a sacred calling. And I vowed on the very day I was sworn into office that all things must cede to prom.

COCO: We actually didn't have a Prom Committee meeting scheduled, which was weird. Everything had pretty much been finalized—I didn't think we had anything left to do but set up the venue on the big night. So I thought something might be wrong. But when we walked into Ms. Segerson's room for Prom Committee, and Bizzy Stanhope was sitting in Avery's seat, I *knew* something was wrong.

MS. SEGERSON: Yes, I let the Prom Committee use my room on the days when it's not occupied by the school newspaper. This isn't a tacit approval of prom as an institution. This is a testament to how stubborn Avery is.
Editor's Note: Thank you, Ms. Segerson. I love you, too.

161

BIZZY STANHOPE: Yes, I had called this emergency meeting of the Prom Committee. Which is why it only made sense that *I* would sit in the chair of power.

TAMSIN BREWER, *best friend of known beelzebufo Bizzy Stanhope*: Bizzy sat in that chair like she was born to sit in it, which she totally was. Everyone knew Bizzy *should* have been head of the Prom Committee. Everyone talked about it, like, all the time.

COCO: The only people who ever talked about Bizzy being head of the Prom Committee were Tamsin and Bizzy. They would whisper furiously about that nonsense idea until Avery silenced them with a look. Pathetic. The only thing worse than insubordination is cowardly insubordination.
   Editor's Note: I would have guessed that was a JFK quote— but it turns out that little gem was pure Coco.

BIZZY: Avery was always late. It was completely unprofessional.

COCO: Avery was only late *sometimes*. And she always had a legitimate excuse.

AVERY: First of all, it is impossible to be late to a meeting you didn't even know was happening until *after* it started. Secondly, the fact that Bizzy had called said meeting was a flagrant slap in the face of my authority. And when I walked in and saw her sitting in my chair—my chair, mind you!—I was *livid*.

MS. SEGERSON: The chair in question is actually *my* chair. Avery somehow convinced me that it was "integral to her authority" that she sit in it. I have an exercise ball I try to sit on after school while grading papers anyway. It's hard to find the time to work out during the school year.

COCO: Bizzy slunk out of the power chair the minute Avery fixed her with a glare. Cowardly insubordination at its worst. Bizzy's attempt to take over this meeting was a total Bay of Pigs, except I wasn't entirely sure who Castro was in this situation, because as much as I hate to admit it, that wasn't Kennedy's finest hour.

AVERY: "Get on with it," I growled at Bizzy's stupid fake-blond head as I resumed my place of pride at the head of the classroom.

BIZZY: Avery is *beyond* rude. None of the Dennises have any manners. There was an incident involving her father and my father on the squash court that could not bear repetition in polite company. Every Dennis in Marin County was banned from the club—in perpetuity.

PAUL DENNIS aka DAD, *father, rage-fueled squash player*: Don't you dare mention the name Ted Stanhope, Avery! You know that man is persona non grata in this house! All I wanted was a competitive game of squash, and instead I have to hear baseless accusations and incessant complaints about how hard it is to steam-clean glitter out of wall-to-wall wool carpeting. And don't get me started on that horrible club and its stringent destruction-of-property policies. If their boilerplate hadn't been so airtight, Dennis, Godfrey & Markham would have sued the khakis off of them.

Editor's Note: To quote a great philosopher: "Never got caught; they take me to the back and pat me."

HUTCH: The more I learned about AD's parents, the more I understood her.

BIZZY: But I brushed aside Avery's rudeness and got right down to business, like the true professional I am. See? This is exactly why *I* should have been head of the Prom Committee.

TAMSIN: Bizzy gave me the signal and I started pushing all of the boxes out of the back of the room and into the center of our Prom Committee circle.

AVERY: I didn't have time for Bizzy's box-based theatrics. I leapt out of my chair, grabbed a pair of scissors off of Ms. Segerson's desk, and cut the box open. Inside, there was a truly horrifying sight. Nothing but hundreds and thousands of brown latex balloons. Brown. Latex. Balloons.

COCO: Avery asked if all of the boxes were filled with brown balloons. Bizzy nodded grimly, but there was something weird about it. Like she was *pretending* to be grim, but not actually grim. I was in Acting 3 with Bizzy last year, so I know all her theatrical tricks. She was doing the same face she did during her Linda Loman monologue from *Death of a Salesman*.

TAMSIN: Yeah, it was my job to order the decorations. Which, honestly, was not the job I wanted, but whatever. I told Avery I was sorry, but I'd ordered the wrong thing. Oh, and I'd spent our whole decorations budget on the balloons. So we didn't have any money left to get anything else.

COCO: Did I suspect sabotage? Absolutely. Immediately. It was painfully obvious that Tamsin was just the front for Bizzy's evil machinations. I wish I could say I didn't believe that Bizzy could stoop so low, but she absolutely would. She would gladly ruin her own prom in order to make Avery look bad. And as much as I truly, deeply dislike Bizzy Stanhope and her lunch-shaming ways, that made me feel kind of sad for her. I couldn't imagine how awful it would be to go through life ruining your own happiness just to make someone else a little unhappier than you are.

AVERY: I had given Tamsin Brewer one job. *One. Job.* How could she possibly have screwed this up?! *Nobody* was that dumb!

TAMSIN: I just got, like, confused by the order numbers. There were so many rows and rows of tiny numbers. It's hard. All numbers look the same to me.

AVERY: Tamsin's "confused by the order numbers" excuse was not an excuse at all. I hadn't even ordered any balloons! It's not like I requested Radiant Orchid balloons and she'd ordered four dozen in Umber instead! These balloons had come out of nowhere! How could she have gotten nothing but brown balloons?

TAMSIN: I didn't *just* get brown balloons. I also got one special one that was a little yellow Minion, like from that movie. Just because I thought he was so cute! I was gonna tie him onto my chair so everybody knew that was where I was sitting, and then we could take pictures together, and I could give him little hugs if I felt sad.

Editor's Note: Obviously, I shouldn't have given Tamsin Brewer any jobs. At this point, I wasn't even sure how she'd made it through high school.

COCO: So here was the situation: We had a thousand hideous brown balloons, and one Minion balloon, but maybe no one but Tamsin was allowed to touch it? It was unclear. I'm not saying that I *wanted* to touch the Minion balloon, but I maybe would have taken a picture with it.

AVERY: Don't even get me started on that stupid Minion balloon. If that tiny yellow nightmare dared show his face at prom, I would stab him in his dumb Mylar face.

COCO: When Avery started threatening to stab cartoon characters, I knew things were bad. Really bad. She had once described the Minions to me as "surprisingly cute—especially the little one." And now she wanted to murder them in balloon form?!

AVERY: Oh, I knew Bizzy was behind it. It was very obvious, from her poorly executed fake sad face and smirk of triumph when she thought nobody was looking. But I am always looking, Bizzy. *I AM ALWAYS LOOKING.*

BIZZY: I was just as shocked as everyone else was. But mostly, I felt bad for poor Tamsin! It was an honest mistake. No one should be shamed for making a very understandable, totally honest mistake. Avery was being completely unforgiving. Again, this is another reason why I should have been head of the Prom Committee. I am way more charitable.

AVERY: We were completely screwed. The prom theme was Midnight in Paris, not Starbucks at Dawn! I had ruined prom. This was how I would go down in history—"Avery Dennis, the girl who ruined San Anselmo Prep's senior prom." They would probably reprint the yearbook so my senior superlative would read *Prom Ruiner* instead of *Most Likely to Take Over the World.* Or maybe they'd just burn a hole in the yearbook where my picture used to be! I'd deserve it!

COCO: We thought that was it. Like, what could be worse than a billion brown balloons? But then Bizzy dropped an even bigger bomb.

AVERY: "Oh," Bizzy said super casually as she examined her scarily sharp manicured nails—seriously, I think she files them into points—"there's a teensy little problem with the venue."

COCO: "What's the problem?" Avery snarled, and never had someone been more deserving of a snarl than Bizzy Stanhope.

AVERY: "They double-booked it," Bizzy said coolly, like she didn't hear my heart drop out of my chest and fall onto the floor.

COCO: Bizzy said, "Sorry," but she didn't sound sorry at all.

BIZZY: It's not my fault that Daddy needed the event space on the exact same night the San Anselmo Prep senior prom just happened to be. What's more important, a corporate merger or a high school dance?

AVERY: I couldn't believe Bizzy. She only had one job to do. One job! The entire reason she was on Prom Committee was because she had secured the venue, except it turned out, the venue wasn't secured at all! In fact, it was nonexistent! There was no venue. Ergo, there was no prom. I had failed as head of the Prom Committee in a way no Prom Committee head had ever failed before. This was worse than when the senior class of 1999 missed out on the obvious opportunity to theme the prom Let's Party Like It's 1999. For the first time since San Anselmo Prep had opened its doors in 1925, there would be no senior prom. And that was all my fault.

COCO: It was absolutely not Avery's fault at all! The only people who were at fault were evil Bizzy Stanhope and her henchman Tamsin.

AVERY: What was I going to do? Move the prom to the gym? With my luck, there was probably a volleyball tournament in there that night. Move the prom to the parking lot? I couldn't think of anywhere to move the prom that didn't fall far short of spectacular, and I knew Bizzy would waste no time telling everyone exactly whose fault it was that we were dancing in a parking lot full of brown balloons.

BIZZY: Listen. Any *good* head of the Prom Committee would have secured a backup venue. Prom was almost definitely canceled, or if it happened, it would be somewhere completely tragic. I couldn't even begin to imagine the things people would say about the formerly golden Avery Dennis and how royally she had screwed up.

AVERY: There was no hope. This would go down in history as the saddest San Anselmo Prep senior prom of all time, and that would be my legacy. People would speak of me in hushed tones for decades to come, like some kind of San Anselmo urban legend.

HUTCH: Avery can be dramatic over the little things—like if the cafeteria doesn't do French Fry Friday, or if she thinks one knee sock is sagging in an unflattering way, or when someone dares to eat raw onions on his cheeseburger, which is a basic human right—but she usually keeps a pretty level head in the face of an actual crisis. You should have seen her spring into action when it looked like Cressida Schrobenhauser-Clonan's team was going to overtake ours on the leaderboard at the Science Olympiad. This is why when she was panicking, actually panicking, about the prom, I knew we had surpassed crisis and shot straight into catastrophe.

AVERY: When Hutch told me he thought he could help, I didn't know *what* to think. How could he possibly save the prom? And why would James "Hutch" Hutcherson, avowed prom hater, even *want* to save the prom? It made absolutely no sense. But I felt like I had no other choice but to place my faith in Hutch. My normally unlimited resourcefulness had abandoned me. I couldn't think of a single thing that could save us from this decorative debacle or a single place we could hold the prom that wasn't tarred in asphalt. I had to accept whatever lifeline I was offered. Even if it came from a scientist who hated dancing.

HUTCH: I had an idea. It was sort of crazy. And it might not have worked. And I definitely had to make some phone calls. And I was worried, beyond worried, that it wouldn't live up to AD's extremely high standards. I had heard AD talk about prom nearly every single day for the past four years. I knew I had to try to save it for her. But I was also terrified that in my attempts to save it, I might ruin prom. But that was a risk I had to take. Like the great Ray Bradbury once said, "Living at risk is jumping off a cliff and building wings on your way down." And I was going to do everything I could to build Avery wings.

Editor's Note: !!!!!?!?!?!!!!! From whence this POETRY, Hutch?!?!

TRIPP GOMEZ-PARKER

AVERY: There was no time to wallow in the unmitigated disaster that was the senior prom. I had to leave it in Hutch's capable hands, trust that he had a miracle up his sleeve, and press on. Prom was only two days away, I had all of my boyfriends from sophomore through senior year to get through, and I *still* didn't have any answers. The project was nowhere near finished, and I felt no closer to reaching enlightenment or understanding!

HUTCH: I had a lot of people to convince and favors to call in if I was going to pull this off. But I couldn't resist weighing in on this particular ex-boyfriend.

COCO: Welcome to Avery's Sophomore Slump.

HUTCH: Is Tripp Gomez-Parker worse than Sean Graney? No, no, I don't think so. Tripp isn't exactly the brightest crayon in the box, but at least he has a neck.

COCO: I know what you're thinking: "Coco, how could you call Tripp Avery's Sophomore Slump? You are literally taking him to the prom in like forty-eight hours." And you would be right about that! But you would only ask that question if you'd never seen him dance. The man is like Channing Tatum in a San Anselmo Prep uniform. And a slightly less muscular body.

TRIPP GOMEZ-PARKER, *ex-boyfriend, lacrosse player, surprisingly proficient dancer*: Whoa, whoa, whoa. Everyone likes to make a big deal about my dancing, but I swear, man, it is no big deal. Dancing is definitely not, like, my *thing*. My thing is lacrosse. If I even have a thing. Do I have a thing? I don't know, man. How would I describe myself in three words? One: male. Two: awesome. Three: lacrosse player.

Editor's Note: Oh, boy.

CRESSIDA SCHROBENHAUSER-CLONAN, *lab partner of T. Gomez-Parker*: Tripp Gomez-Parker has been a carbuncle on my sterling GPA all year. I can obviously carry his deadweight and *still* beat out Hutcherson to become valedictorian, but it's been slightly more challenging than it otherwise would have been. So maybe I should thank Tripp for keeping things interesting. And for finally learning not to eat erasers.

TRIPP: Hold up—Cressida said what? Man, I only ate an eraser one time! And it was shaped like a tiny watermelon. Probable cause, yo! There's a reason erasers should be shaped like erasers.

HUTCH: There is no way Cressida is beating me for valedictorian. She'd best be writing her salutation right now.

CRESSIDA: Obviously, if Hutch and I had been allies instead of enemies, there was no telling how high our GPAs could have climbed. If only Avery Dennis hadn't kept us apart . . . well. A lot of things might have happened.

Editor's Note: OMG, obsessed much, Cressida? If I'd known she was that desperate to be Hutch's lab partner . . . well, I still probably wouldn't have given him up, honestly.

COCO: I love talking about when Avery and Tripp dated. She is *constantly* trying to talk me out of taking him to prom, and this is literally the only thing that will shut her up! After all, Tripp and I are most emphatically *not* dating. He is not my boyfriend. We are not a couple. We are going to the prom together, and that is absolutely it. So if anyone deserves to be teased about her relationship with Tripp—even a former one—it's Avery.

TRIPP: When Avery started asking me all these questions about sophomore year, I started getting mad nervous. But she promised—pinky-promised—that no one but her and Ms. Segerson would ever read this thing.

HUTCH: When AD told me I couldn't listen in on her conversation with Tripp, I was confused. But then I remembered that she didn't know that I know . . . you know what? Never mind. I respected her space and headed off to try to save the prom. Man, that's not something I ever thought I'd say.

Editor's Note: Mysterious much, Hutch? Whatever, I needed his help.

COCO: No, I wasn't there when Avery and Tripp started dating. That's weird, right? She just walked into school one day and boom, she was Tripp's girlfriend.

AVERY: Somehow, Dad felt like I needed even more extracurriculars—I swear it's like he didn't want me to ever have any time for anything else but school. Luckily, I knew exactly what else I wanted to do. Not a lot of people know this, but Audrey Hepburn was also a classically trained ballerina who danced professionally—and that's why I decided to start taking ballet sophomore year. Audrey Hepburn started dancing when she was five. Unfortunately, so did the rest of the world, apparently. It was super hard to find a beginning ballet class for teens. All the teen classes were at the, like, triple advanced level! So I ended up finding a dance studio, way far away in a whole different town, that had a Beginning Teen/Adult class.

TRIPP: I thought I had been crazy careful. Why would anyone from San Anselmo be at a dance class in Petaluma? It's like forty minutes away.

AVERY: I was pulling on my pink ballet slippers, trying to decide how I felt about being the only teen in the adults/teen class—would it be beyond awkward? Or would I learn lots of great Pinterest recipes for the crockpot I would someday own? That's what I always assume adults talk about. Then, I saw the last person I would expect to see walk out of the Teen Triple Advanced Ballet Ninja class or whatever it was called.

TRIPP: My heart stopped. I thought there was a legit chance I'd vom all over the studio. Was Avery the absolute worst person to run into at Madame Dubonnet's? Maybe not the *worst*, but she was pretty high up there on my list of "worst people to run into." Bizzy Stanhope would have been worse, for sure. Or Sean Graney. Or Tamsin Brewer. But Avery was not a great person to run into. At least I was wearing track pants over my dance tights.

MADAME DUBONNET, *former ABT principal dancer, owner of Madame Dubonnet's School of Dance in Petaluma*: Tripp has studied with me since he was very young. His mother brought him to class when he was only four years old because his older sister was in my studio, but it became apparent to me that Tripp was the Gomez-Parker sibling with talent. He has been with our school of dance ever since, and although I do not think he has the technique to dance professionally, he is, without a doubt, very gifted.

TRIPP: Dag, I thought, my secret double life was over. No doubt Avery was going to make fun of me. And tell everyone at school what she saw. And then I'd become a total reject and have to eat lunch every day with Hutch and Michael Feeley and those guys. Not that they're total rejects, but, uh . . . You know what I mean.

AVERY: I couldn't stop staring. The adult beginning ballerinas were pushing their way around me to get into the studio, but

I couldn't move! I just stood and stared at Tripp, with my jaw hanging open.

TRIPP: Avery was mad horrified. She couldn't even speak! She just stood there staring at me. I was bugging. So I tried to get ready to spend the rest of high school known as Ballet Boy.

AVERY: It explained a lot, though. It really did. Tripp is—was—a great dancer. At every dance we've had since sixth grade, a dance circle has formed around him at some point. There's no way that was *just* natural talent. Some of those skills were taught. And taught well, by Madame Dubonnet.

MADAME DUBONNET: Ah, yes, Mademoiselle Dennis, I remember that one. She does not have grace, of any kind. Her movements are so forceful. I feared, always, for my beautiful floors when she pirouetted across them. When she began her relationship with my star, Tripp, I was astonished. How could two creatures who were so different relate to one another in any way? It was like a bull dating a butterfly.

Editor's Note: I cannot believe I am not the butterfly in this simile. I also can't believe Tripp Gomez-Parker is the butterfly in this simile. Also, she'd just called us "creatures."

AVERY: There was a lot I didn't—don't—understand about Tripp. The guy is, objectively, an idiot. I feel like I constantly have to be on guard about him groping Coco. And yet . . . There was something about him when he danced. Something, perhaps, that revealed a more sensitive soul.

TRIPP: That first day I saw Avery in the ballet studio, I just walked past her. Straight-up ghosted. I couldn't talk to her. I didn't know what to say—what *could* I say?! When I walked into school the following morning, I was mad nervous. I waited for the haters to start chanting "Ballet Boy," but I never heard anything. School was chill! Avery hadn't told anyone. I couldn't believe it.

AVERY: No, I didn't tell anyone. I thought about telling Coco—*obviously*, I thought about telling Coco. This was probably the craziest thing I'd found out about a classmate since I discovered that Tamsin Brewer was so good at making balloon animals she was basically a professional clown—but somehow I just couldn't do it. The way Tripp looked at me when he saw me see him . . . no. I couldn't do it. He just looked so . . . scared. And broken, almost. Defeated.

TRIPP: I didn't know why Avery didn't blow me up, but I had to talk to her. Beginning Teen/Adult Ballet meets Tuesdays and Thursdays at Madame Dubonnet's. I hung around after Tuesday night class until Avery got out.

MADAME DUBONNET: The second week of beginning ballet, Mademoiselle Dennis still had not mastered the positions of the feet. I knew there was no hope for her.

AVERY: Week two of ballet was basically amazing. I was pretty confident I had a gift. But I hadn't seen Tripp on my way into class, so I was assuming he was going to hide from me forever and pretend the whole thing had never happened. I mean, that's probably what I would have done if I had run into Tripp if I was at, oh, I don't know, pro wrestling practice? Or maybe I would be proud because that actually sounds kind of awesome? Anyway. I was very surprised when I got out of class and saw Tripp waiting on a bench in the studio's entryway, with two Styrofoam cups of hot herbal tea—what a healthy choice! The Tripp Gomez-Parker I thought I knew only drank the weird punch they have in the cafeteria and Monster energy drinks.

TRIPP: I told Avery everything. All of it. The grueling hours rehearsing at the barre, the long drives to competition, and how I'd been crushing ballet since I was just a cute li'l baby Tripp.

AVERY: I couldn't believe what I was hearing. Our grade's resident hot idiot was a dedicated, passionate, classically trained ballerina? Er, ballet man? It seemed impossible, and yet here he was, sitting in front of me in a Madame Dubonnet's School of Dance Competition Team hoodie. It made absolutely no sense.

TRIPP: Do I remember when I realized I should be embarrassed by ballet? Naw, man. I just always knew that if I said anything, I'd get a patented Sean Graney wedgie.

AVERY: In one way, though, it *did* make sense. Tripp has seriously gnarly feet. They are *beyond* disgusting. Like all cut up and blistered and bruised and weird. Honestly, they look like big, horrifyingly bruised pieces of rotten fruit. Too graphic? Anyway. Once he went mini golfing with me and Coco and everyone, and I legit almost threw up on the ninth hole because he was wearing flip-flops.

TRIPP: After I told her everything about ballet, I expected . . . well, I don't know what I expected. What I definitely *didn't* expect was that Avery would kiss me.

AVERY: A kiss seemed like the only appropriate response! The guy had just bared his soul, for Pete's sake! I didn't kiss Tripp because I felt *bad* for him or anything, he just looked so vulnerable and sweet—so *different* from the Tripp I thought I knew—that I couldn't help myself. I leaned in, and he was definitely surprised, but he wasn't surprised for long. When he put his hands on my waist, I imagined him lifting me through the air, like we were doing the Act III pas de deux from *Sleeping Beauty*.

MADAME DUBONNET: No, no, Mademoiselle Dennis could not handle partner work. She most definitely could never be the Sleeping Beauty! It is appalling to consider.

Editor's Note: Well, there goes my ballet career. But also, I haven't taken a ballet class in two years, and I definitely left a lasting impression on Madame Dubonnet. So there's that. I may not be a good dancer, but at least I'm an unforgettable one. She remembered more about me than Bobby Boback did.

TRIPP: I had spent a lot of time in that dance studio since elementary school. Lots of good memories. When I did my first lift. When I first nailed a grand jeté. When I found out I was playing the Nutcracker Prince in our annual company Christmas show. But the moment Avery kissed me is definitely mad high on that list of good dance studio memories.

MADAME DUBONNET: I knew that girl would be no good for my Tripp. If he had taken up with one of my principals, fine. I have seen it happen before, many times, where the intimacy of partner work bleeds into a relationship of a romantic nature outside the studio. But I knew Mademoiselle Dennis would be nothing but a distraction. We were mere months away from *The Nutcracker,* and I could not afford to have my Prince lose his focus.

COCO: The Avery and Tripp thing came literally out of nowhere. Seriously. The last text I got from her said, "LOL this leotard, though >" with a selfie and a bunch of emojis. Does that sound like, "Hey, best friend Coco, I have a new boyfriend!"? No. No, it does not. Not that Avery needs to clear her entire life with me, but it's a little embarrassing when *Bizzy Stanhope* knows your best friend is in a new relationship before you do.

BIZZY STANHOPE, *still the worst but somehow keeps being relevant, which is absolutely murdering me right now*: I was the first person who saw Avery and Tripp together. Was I surprised? Not particularly. Who *hasn't* Avery Dennis dated, after all? She can't hold on to a boyfriend, so she constantly needs a new one. She'll work her way through the entire dating pool eventually. Well, I guess she did . . . and that's how you end up sad and lonely with no prom date. Tripp and Avery travel in the same circles, they go to the same parties, they eat at the same table . . . It seemed pretty logical. The only thing that *was* surprising was that it had *seemed* like, for years and years and years, that Tripp had been into Coco. Which would lead one to assume that, in some way, even some small way, Coco was into Tripp. And yet . . . Coco's very best friend had swooped in right under her nose and stolen him. It was a classic Avery Dennis move.

COCO: What?! No! No!! She said *what*?! I am not—was not—will never be—*into* Tripp Gomez-Parker. Listen. The only reason I was upset—and *upset* is too strong a word, really—when Avery started dating Tripp was because I like to know these things before the rest of the school does. That is all.

Editor's Note: Oh, no. Oh God, no. The lady doth protest too much, methinks! Could Coco actually be into Tripp?! If Coco has been carrying a secret torch for Tripp since kindergarten and never told me, I will be devastated. Especially if it turns out I screwed things up for her by kissing him in a dance studio sophomore year. But do I even want Coco to be into Tripp? Ugh, talking about sophomore year was making me remember Tripp's sensitive side and forget all of his bad parts. I couldn't let my guard down about Tripp and Coco. Constant vigilance! I would not let my best friend get busted for inappropriate dancing like she was some kind of Bizzy Stanhope.

BIZZY: The whole thing was just very basic. Everyone kept eating at the same lunch tables. Everyone still did the same things on the weekend. I don't think they even spent that much time together outside of school. You could hardly call it a relationship.

AVERY: Tripp and I spent all our time outside of school together at Madame Dubonnet's. Mostly because I quickly discovered that Tripp spent every waking moment he wasn't at school or at sports practice in the ballet studio. Obviously, I couldn't keep up with him on the dance floor, but I could stretch and do my homework and stuff while Madame Dubonnet drilled him and he trained with the teenage girls who were actually good. God, this was just like Ben and Grapenuts all over again. Underclassman Avery had a real problem with spending all her free time watching her boyfriends do things.

TRIPP: It was awesome having Avery at the studio. I'd never been able to hang out there with someone I went to school with before! And she could help with my homework. That was like the only semester in high school I wasn't even close to failing. Avery is crazy smart. I feel like that's something not a lot of people know about her.

COCO: Why did Tripp and Avery break up? You know what? I can't remember. Huh. That's weird. They dated for kind of a while, too—like almost four months. You'd think the breakup would have been more dramatic.

HUTCH: I assumed Avery broke up with Tripp because she actually talked to him. Sorry—that was mean. He's not a bad guy; he's really not. He postures a lot—he's got that faux-cool-guy swagger—but I've never heard him be actively cruel, like Sean Graney or some of the other guys in the popular circle. But he's certainly not someone I would describe as an intellectual. A nice guy, but dim.

CRESSIDA: I've said it before and I'll say it again—Tripp Gomez-Parker is as dumb as a box of rocks.

AVERY: Tripp and I broke up because I wanted him to go public, and he wouldn't.

TRIPP: Avery tried to ruin me.

AVERY: Let me clarify—we were public about our relationship. I wanted him to go public about what an amazing dancer he was. He was hiding this whole huge part of himself because he was scared! And he had *nothing* to be scared about. I know he was worried people would make fun of him, but I thought it would make people like him *more*. I know it made me like him more. He was so talented, and so strong—a real athlete. I thought that if people saw how cool ballet actually was, and how awesome Trip was, they would understand. Why were we living in a cultural prison of outdated gender norms?! It was time for freedom!

TRIPP: I don't think any of this had anything to do with me. Avery wanted me to go public because she wanted people to see her in *The Nutcracker*.

MADAME DUBONNET: Every student in my school is guaranteed a role in our Christmas production of *The Nutcracker*. Usually, my beginning adult and teen students do not audition. Unfortunately for me, however, Mademoiselle Dennis did audition, and I was left with no choice but to cast her.

AVERY: When Tripp said my motives for him coming clean were purely selfish, it hurt. A lot. *Obviously*, I wanted people from school to come see me in *The Nutcracker*. Of course I did! It's not every day that you get to play a male child, a rat, and a gingerbread cookie—a horrifying list of garbage roles I was somehow proud of—and I wanted my peers to see me shine! I was the only gingerbread cookie who was over the age of seven. I wanted people to see me tromp around the stage as the largest cookie in *Nutcracker* history! And let's not disregard the Coco factor. If I told Coco I *didn't* want her to come see my ballet debut, she would be instantly suspicious. I mean, I made Coco come to the time I debuted the fact that I could do a handstand, and that was in my backyard.

COCO: Oh, sure, yeah, I remember Avery's handstand debut! The refreshments were quite good.

AVERY: But just because I wanted people to see me dance my ratty little heart out on the stage doesn't mean that was the *only* reason I wanted Tripp to tell everyone about who he really was.

TRIPP: I should have seen this coming the minute the *Nutcracker* cast list went up at Madame Dubonnet's and Avery was so stoked about being a rat—which is also bizarre, like who ever is really stoked about being a rat—but I can be really slow sometimes.

COCO: Avery was soooo excited about doing *The Nutcracker*. She was asking me all these questions about rat makeup versus gingerbread makeup, and if I thought she could convincingly play a boy in the party scene, and did I think they would let her wear a beanie, because although it was set in the nineteenth century, she felt that a beanie was really integral to her character.

Editor's Note: My character in the party scene was a troubled young man named Johann. Madame Dubonnet was really resistant to a lot of my choices, but that's the

problem with these classical French ballet mistresses—
they're stuck in the past, unable to see the vision of the
next generation.

TRIPP: It hit me really embarrassingly late in the rehearsal process. Wasn't until costume fittings. Avery was dancing around
in her gingerbread outfit, super pissing off Madame Dubonnet,
who requires that people remain in the dressing room during
fittings, not on the studio floor, when she said, "I can't wait
until Coco sees this!" And it was like every blood cell in my
body turned to ice.

AVERY: I caught Tripp's eyes in the mirror where I was
admiring my own reflection and knew something was wrong.
Madame Dubonnet caught me and hauled me back to the
dressing room. Tripp waited outside, and the minute I changed
out of my gingerbread suit, he told me I absolutely, positively,
could not invite anyone from school to see *The Nutcracker.*

TRIPP: It wasn't possible. No way. No way, man! I look a little
different with my stage makeup, but not different enough. Plus,
my name would be right there in the program! And, like, don't
get me wrong, Coco's mad chill, but even just having Avery
know my secret felt like too many people. I couldn't let it
spread. And the odds of Avery only inviting one person from
school seemed pretty dang slim. I was surprised she hadn't
already taken out an ad in the school newspaper.

AVERY: At first, I was outraged. How dare he tell me what to do! I'm an independent woman! I make my own guest list, thank you very much!

TRIPP: I begged her. I pleaded. There was definitely some groveling involved. It was not my manliest moment. You ever see a dude in dance tights grovel? It's not pretty.

AVERY: It broke my heart, a little. But I'm not a monster. It would have been unforgivably selfish to make a decision that, like it or not, would have impacted Tripp's life, too. So I promised that I wouldn't invite anyone from school. And then we broke up. We wanted different things—I wanted people to come see the show, and he didn't. I couldn't live his secret double life anymore. I was proud to be a ballerina's girlfriend, and if he couldn't be proud, too, then I couldn't be his girlfriend.

MADAME DUBONNET: That year, Tripp danced the Nutcracker Prince as though he danced for his soul. There was an anguish he brought to the piece that gave it a depth one does not usually associate with *The Nutcracker*. It remains one of his finest performances, and, perhaps, my favorite *Nutcracker*. So perhaps I have Mademoiselle Dennis to thank after all. A bit of heartbreak is good for a dancer. Mademoiselle Dennis's performance? Ah, she managed not to ruin the party scene or the gingerbread dance, and actually made a somewhat convincing rat.

Editor's Note: I knew I'd win her over eventually with my ratty skills! Also, I definitely did not break Tripp's heart—I am not nearly conceited enough to think his anguished dancing had anything to do with me. That was all the torture of his secret double life.

COCO: I felt so bad for Avery. It was the craziest freak accident! The pipes burst in the theater, and they canceled the production of *The Nutcracker*! It was all she'd been talking about for weeks, and then the show just didn't happen. Isn't that awful? You would think they would have been able to find an alternate space or something, but Avery said the sets were just too elaborate to re-create on such short notice. And then Tripp broke up with her—or she broke up with him? I don't remember, exactly. Anyway, it was a very sad December. We had a lot of cocoa.

HUTCH: Avery came into school and spent the entire day talking very, very loudly about how the pipes burst in the theater and *The Nutcracker* was canceled. Something seemed off about the whole thing. When I asked her a question about how the water in the pipes could have possibly gotten close to freezing—pipes usually burst because water expands as it freezes, which causes an increase of pressure inside the pipe, which ruptures them—she got all shifty and clammed up. I pointed out that the temperature hadn't dropped below 49 degrees all month, and she said, and I quote, "Shut it, Hutch, you're not a pipe doctor," which is when I definitely knew she was lying.

AVERY: Stupid Hutch and his stupid rational mind! He stopped poking around after I told him to shut it, but I was still nervous he'd accidentally expose Tripp. Of course I wanted Tripp to tell everyone who he really was, but I wanted him to do it on his own terms, not because I'd forced him to.

HUTCH: The crazy thing to me is that nobody at our school even bothered to google it. Seems completely obvious, right? I guess everyone just took Avery at her word. But I went to Madame Dubonnet's website. They were still selling tickets— no mention of burst pipes anywhere to be found.

AVERY: And you know what? It ended up being totally fine that Coco and everyone else from school couldn't come. Honestly, I looked like a big old idiot in that cookie costume, so it was probably better that no one but my mom and dad saw me. Dad's review: "Christ, Avery, that was long." Mom's review: "You make a surprisingly convincing rat." So I pretty much nailed it.

PAUL DENNIS aka DAD, *father, ballet hater*: Avery, I wasn't saying you did a bad job when I said the show was long! Long is good! Great, even! It was just . . . It was really long, kid.

HUTCH: I knew that blond "boy" in the party scene was Avery. I spotted her right away. But I didn't understand why she'd told everyone the show was canceled until the Nutcracker came to life. At first, I couldn't believe what I was seeing. I figured I had to be wrong—it was just someone who *looked* almost identical to Tripp Gomez-Parker. Tripp, in a ballet? Tripp, *good* at ballet? It seemed impossible, but the most logical explanation is, after all, usually the right one. This explained why Avery had kept everyone from our school from coming to the show. Tripp must not have been ready for people to know he was into ballet. Although I don't know *why*, because the guy was incredible. I had come to see Avery, obviously, but I felt like I spent most of the show staring at Tripp with my jaw hanging open, rubbing my eyes in disbelief.

Editor's Note: WHAT?! Hutch came and saw The Nutcracker?! *Why did he come?? Why did he never tell me that he came?? What did this even mean?!*

HUTCH: I never told anyone what I'd seen. Liam probably could have kept it a secret, but Alex would have had a field day—could you imagine? He's always getting worked up over the popular kids. Probably would have tried to bring Tripp down in some kind of *Revenge of the Nerds* ballet maneuver. If AD wanted to keep Tripp's secret, then I'd keep it for her, too.

TRIPP: Avery Dennis is a really cool girl, man. I don't think there are a lot of people who could have kept that to themselves. Usually nothing is a secret at San Anselmo Prep. But she really kept that one on lockdown. Do I think I'll ever tell anyone? Maybe. Yeah, maybe in college. Things'll be different in college, I bet. The dance department at my school's supposed to be pretty good. I've been thinking about trying out for the fall show. The girls in the pictures on the website are smoking.

Editor's Note: Ugh. See? Still the same old Tripp.

HUTCH: And you know what? Avery was a really good rat.

EZRA DIRKS

AVERY: For the last boyfriend in the sophomore slump, there's really nothing *that* wrong with Ezra Dirks.

COCO: There are two things that are very wrong with Ezra: his parents.

HUTCH: In 1990, childhood development researchers Foster Cline and Jim Fay coined the term *helicopter parent* to describe parents who "hover"—hence the helicopter—over their children in a way that inhibits the child's development into an independent adult. I have no evidence to support my theory that they coined this term after meeting Joan and Martin Dirks, but I certainly wouldn't be surprised if they had. Ezra and I don't even have any classes together, and I'm on a first-name basis with both of his parents. I think that shows you just how involved they are.

PRINCIPAL PATEL, *principal*: We have a great deal of parental involvement here at San Anselmo Prep, but they are some parents who take the term *involvement* to a whole new level. No, no, it's a good thing! Of course it's a good thing! I so enjoy my weekly phone check-ins with Mrs. Dirks on Ezra's progress.
Editor's Note: It did not sound like he enjoyed it.

TRIPP GOMEZ-PARKER: I think most people know who Ezra Dirks is because his mom still walks him all the way *inside* the building to make sure he can open his locker. For the first week of school, she sits in the back of all his classes, too, and she makes sure he can transition from class to class. I'm serious, man. She even did it this year. Senior year! Can you imagine what happens next year when Ezra goes to college? His mom's probably gonna enroll and make sure she's his roommate.

EZRA DIRKS, *ex-boyfriend, helicopter child*: People like to make a big deal about my mom, but it's really not a big deal. It's not. She just likes to be involved in my life. It's not that weird.

BIZZY STANHOPE: Ezra is *so* weird. His parents are obsessed with him. He's basically a giant baby. I'm surprised he and Avery didn't date for longer, considering that she's also a giant baby. She's still throwing a temper tantrum about the fact that we lost our venue due to an unforeseeable financial situation. It's like, get over it. The only person you have to blame is yourself. What kind of subpar head of the Prom Committee doesn't have a Plan B when it comes to the venue anyway? I hope everyone remembers this when casting their votes for Prom Queen. Well, on the big night, I'll make sure everyone knows *exactly* whose fault it is. If it even happens.

> *Editor's Note: Evil. Pure evil. When I asked Principal Patel if we could hypothetically move the prom to the parking lot, he said okay but that the school would not provide any tables*

and wouldn't be liable for people falling on the asphalt. Then he started asking all these questions about why I would even want to hypothetically move the prom to a parking lot, and I felt like such a failure, I couldn't tell him what had happened, so I mumbled something about the infinite nature of possibility and left. I really hope Hutch has a miracle planned. Because that's the only thing that can save us now.

COCO: It's just hitting me now that I should have been doing a better job of policing post-breakup Avery. Not just sophomore year—our whole lives! She's always extremely vulnerable to a new relationship in the wake of the old one's demise. Sometimes I think it's like Puck flew in and hit her with that magic love flower like in A *Midsummer Night's Dream*—she pretty much starts dating the next moderately cute guy she sees. Although I probably couldn't have done much. Avery's dad has been clearly trying to keep Avery too busy to date for years. Look how unsuccessful that's been, and Paul Dennis once had an entire airport shut down.

Editor's Note: It was a small airfield, but still.

EZRA: Avery Dennis literally ran into me.

COCO: Avery has two modes in school—she either forgets everything she needs or she carries the entire contents of her locker with her. The Ezra Dirks day was an entire-contents-of-the-locker day.

EZRA: Avery collided with me, and her papers exploded all over the hall. Reams of papers filled with notes in a rainbow of pen colors. I bent down to help her pick them up, and our eyes connected while we were on the floor.

AVERY: A shock of brown hair fell into his eyes in a very charming way. And then he stood up to hand me my papers, and I'd forgotten that Ezra Dirks was really very tall. Surprisingly tall. Pleasingly tall. So what if his mom walked him inside? Maybe it was nice that he liked his mom! I asked him out.

COCO: It always happens when I least expect it. I mean, seriously—Ezra Dirks? His most distinguishing characteristic is his *mom*. That's not exactly a vote of confidence in Ezra as a person slash potential boyfriend.

AVERY: I knew that Ezra's parents were involved in his life, but my parents are involved in my life, too! Parents are simply a factor in any relationship when you're a lowly high schooler. Besides, I thought I would have been used to it from hanging out with Coco. Her parents are pretty protective, so I honestly didn't think it would be that different.

COCO: My parents are *nothing* like the Dirkses. My mom didn't want me to go to Italy because she thought someone might pinch my butt. Ezra's parents don't like him to cross the street by himself.

JOAN DIRKS, *helicopter mom*: I'm always surprised that Ezra hasn't had more girlfriends. He's intelligent, kind, funny, handsome, sensitive . . . a total catch.

MARTIN DIRKS, *helicopter dad*: Of course, Ezra has always been very focused on his studies. Doesn't leave a lot of time to date when you're conducting graduate-level work in high school!
Editor's Note: Hutch choked on his lemonade when he heard that bit about "graduate-level work."

MRS. DIRKS: I remember Avery, though. Very pretty. Very polite when we picked her up for their first date.

AVERY: I didn't think anything of it when the Dirks family minivan rolled up in front of my house. After all, we were sophomores—drivers' licenses were thin on the ground. I happily clambered into the back with Ezra, thinking his parents were going to drop us off at the movie theater. But then they parked.

MRS. DIRKS: No, I certainly wouldn't feel comfortable with Ezra seeing a movie without me, especially not with someone I didn't know very well. I was sure Avery was a very nice girl, but you never know, do you?
Editor's Note: I really wish she had elaborated. What did she think I was going to do?! Shank him with a shiv I'd fashioned out of a straw if he hogged the popcorn?

EZRA: My parents prefer that I only watch movies that are rated PG, which is totally fine by me. A lot of directors use language, nudity, and violence as crutches, anyway. You really have to rely on the storytelling when you're crafting a film to fit within the confines of the strictest subset of the ratings system.

AVERY: When Ezra suggested we see the new Pixar movie, of course I was happy to go! I've got eyes, ears, and a heart, don't I? Who doesn't love Pixar?! I didn't realize, however, that Ezra had made his choice out of necessity. I didn't find out until later that he was only allowed to watch PG-rated movies.

COCO: When Avery texted me that Ezra's parents were coming into the movie theater with them, I thought, okay, maybe they're buying the popcorn. When she texted me that they followed them into the theater, I thought, okay, well, my mom sat in the back of the theater when I went out with Sam Levi in eighth grade. But when she texted me that Ezra's mom sat *between* her and Ezra, I knew we were on a whole different level.

AVERY: She chirped, "Let's sit girls and boys!" and maneuvered me away from her precious son. Thank God I had gotten M&M's, because my popcorn access was almost nil.

COCO: This was the red flag to end all red flags. This was Enjolras building a barricade in the back of the movie theater so he could stand on it and wave that huge *Les Miz* red flag. And yet . . . Avery ignored it.

MRS. DIRKS: It was great, getting to sit with Avery at the movies. I could tell she really enjoyed our girl time!

EZRA: My mom and Avery got along really well. It was awesome.

COCO: You know what? Maybe the Sophomore Slump had nothing to do with the guys. I think it was literally Avery's Sophomore Slump—like Avery was the one in a slump, not the duds she picked. The Avery I know today would have demanded to sit next to Ezra, and then probably dumped him in the parking lot for not demanding to sit next to her. But sophomore Avery let this relationship drag on *forever*. Months. Seriously! Months! It went on until the end of sophomore year!

AVERY: Nothing Ezra or his parents did was ever really that bad, you know? Ezra was really sweet, and if I had to spend a lot of time with his mom, well . . . Joan wasn't that bad either.

COCO: Finally, it was the steak that broke the camel's back.

MR. DIRKS: We decided to take Ezra out to dinner to celebrate his tremendous accomplishment of graduation from sophomore year—what a seminal year! Ezra invited Avery along to dinner at the steakhouse as well, and we were happy to have her.

AVERY: I love a good steak. New York strip, medium rare, baked potato on the side . . . I'm in. I was happily chowing down when I noticed something very, very wrong.

MRS. DIRKS: The knives seemed awfully sharp, and the steak was much bigger than I had thought it would be. So I started cutting Ezra's steak into bites for him, like I always do, and blowing on the pieces to cool them down. They were much too hot.

AVERY: HIS MOM WAS CUTTING HIS MEAT. HE WAS A FIFTEEN-YEAR-OLD MAN-BOY WHOSE MOM CUT HIS MEAT FOR HIM. I had to get out of there. I had already stayed in that relationship far, far too long.

EZRA: I have no idea what freaked Avery out at the steakhouse. I guess she's kind of crazy. She stood up, said, "We're done here," grabbed her steak, and walked out of the restaurant.

MR. DIRKS: It's always the pretty ones who are nuts, huh? Girls just can't help themselves around Ezra—they go crazy for him. I guess Avery couldn't handle the magnitude of his charisma.

AVERY: I hope Ezra's mom has a fantastic time at our parking-lot prom.

MRS. DIRKS: I knew it from the very beginning, and I'll say it again now—Ezra was too good for her. It's so hard for Ezra to find someone who really, truly deserves him.

PAUL DENNIS aka DAD, *father, reluctant chauffeur*: Pam was at her book club, so I had to come pick Avery up at Le Steak when she called. I found her sitting in the parking lot, eating a New York strip with a couple of the busboys. That was the moment I knew things had gone too far. Dennises don't eat steaks in parking lots, for Christ's sake! The only time we eat in parking lots is during tailgates, and there was no tailgate here. Avery's obsession with dating had to be stopped—and fast.

COCO: My God, reliving the Sophomore Slump had been rough. I was so ready to move on to junior year.

HUTCH: What was the lesson here? I couldn't figure out why on earth AD would have agreed to go out with any of these guys.

AVERY: I knew exactly what the lesson was—that I had made the right decision by vowing to stay single. What was I missing out on by giving up dating? Sharing popcorn with someone's mom? I could share popcorn with my own mom.

HUTCH: And then I had a major lightbulb moment. We knew AD had been the instigator of most of her relationships. But when she wasn't . . . had AD ever actually turned down anyone who had asked her out?

COCO: You know . . . Wow. You know what? I don't think Avery's ever actually said no to anyone who asked her out. Isn't that crazy? I tell people *no* all the time. I'm like a *no* machine!

BIZZY: Of course Avery's never turned anyone down. Dennises are desperate. That's what Daddy says. They're desperate in business deals, and they're desperate in dating.

Editor's Note: NO ONE calls Dennises desperate! Bizzy was ripe for another shoe full of glitter.

HUTCH: This was fascinating. AD *looks* like the popular girl from a movie who would laugh in a guy's face when he asked her out—I know that's not who she is, but that's who she looks like. I had a theory, though, as to why AD had had so many boyfriends—and it was so much more than simply her never turning anyone down. It explained, I thought, why *she* was almost always the person doing the asking out. I think AD likes to see the best in people. I think she likes to give everyone a shot. I think she sees parts of people they don't normally show anyone else—I don't think it was a coincidence that she was the only person in our grade Tripp Gomez-Parker had ever been totally honest with about his secret life, even if her showing up at the ballet studio seems like a completely random event. There's something about AD that makes people feel okay to be completely themselves. She'd asked all these guys out because she'd seen something great in them, even if it was something they couldn't see themselves. Plus, I think she's way more a hopeless romantic than she'd want you to think.

I think AD always thinks her next boyfriend is going to be "the one."

Editor's Note: That was a lot of I thinks, Hutch! Am I all those things? Do I make people feel those things?! I felt like the more Hutch was analyzing me, maybe the more I was actually learning about Hutch. Like how kind he was, and how generous he was with his opinions of other people. Of me. Hutch showed me far more kindness than I'd shown to so many of my ex-boyfriends. I was still feeling bad about Liam Padalecki. ☹

THE COWBOY

AVERY: The slump was finally over, but it was busted in the most unlikely of places—the quarantine center where my dad forced us to spend the summer to keep me away from boys.

PAUL DENNIS aka DAD, *father, boyfriend hater*: All of Avery's little romantic entanglements had been cute when she was ten. I didn't mind the handmade valentines and misspelled poems cluttering up our fridge. I didn't even mind driving her to the putt-putt course or the movie theater or wherever her current swain was taking her. But as Avery finished sophomore year, it became abundantly clear to me that boys had become nothing but a distraction, and it was time for Avery to get serious. You couldn't put down "serial dating" as an extracurricular activity on a college application.

PAMELA DENNIS aka MOM, *mother, accomplice*: I hadn't thought of any of Avery's boyfriends as a *problem*, per se, as her grades held steady, but even I could see that they were taking up an awful lot of time. Besides, when Paul proposed a family trip to a dude ranch, I thought it sounded like a real hoot! I couldn't even remember a time Paul had spent that much time away from the office.

DAD: Little Lazy River Dude Ranch has excellent Wi-Fi and cell service. I set up a satellite office and kept Dennis, Godfrey & Markham running like a well-oiled machine.

AVERY: When Dad told me we were spending the whole summer on a family trip, I thought he'd lost it. What happened to all of those extracurriculars and internships I needed for my college application? But when Dad told me we were spending the summer *in Texas*, I *knew* he'd lost it.

DAD: I'd tried to keep Avery busy over the years with extracurricular activities; colleges do look at all of that when making their decisions. But don't count out old Dad. I might seem crazy. But it's crazy like a fox.

    Editor's Note: What does crazy like a fox even mean? I asked Hutch if foxes had a tendency toward mental illness, and his answer was an emphatic no.

KRISSY VALDEZ, *Managing Director of Little Lazy River Dude Ranch*: There is technically no age limit in our Big Buckaroo program. I'd say the vast majority of families show up with kids under twelve. Usually, our Big Buckaroos top out around thirteen. But every once in a while, we'll get an outlier.

AVERY: Dad signed up me for ranch camp. For babies. On the surface of the sun.

COCO: While I was decorating my intern desk at the JFK Presidential Library in Boston, the first postcard arrived from

Avery. On the front was a picture of the most adorable little blond boy riding the cutest, fattest pony I'd ever seen. On the back, all it said was *"SEND HELP."*

MOM: Little Lazy River Dude Ranch has so many wonder-ful activities, for both parents and children. On our very first day, I signed Paul and myself up for the Cactus Talk, the Nature Walk, and Watercolor Class. Avery was enrolled in Big Buckaroos with the rest of the big kids.

AVERY: I'd like to think that Mom was ignorant of the fact that she sent me to horseback riding camp with a bunch of tweens. Dad, however, knew exactly what he was doing.

DAD: Oh, I was proud of myself, all right. Thought I'd solved Avery's dating problem by cutting her off at the source. How was she going to find a date when she was spending every day surrounded by middle schoolers?

AVERY: It was humiliating. There were twelve of us Big Buckaroos, and the next oldest one was a thirteen-year-old named Kyra, who was more than willing to be my new BFF. Riding around all day in the summer heat of Texas was exactly the nightmare it sounded like. I smelled like a horse and I couldn't stop sweating. I felt like our counselor, Miss Molly, was laughing at me the whole time. I was ninety-nine percent sure she was only a year or two older than me.

DAD: One week went by with no boyfriend. Then two. Then three. It was the longest stretch I could remember Avery being single. My plan had worked. Sure, she was grumpy and the horse stench coming off her was appalling, but she was plowing her way through that summer reading list.

AVERY: Dad had bested me. I resigned myself to a summer of French-braiding Kyra's hair and bonding with my horse, Li'l Chunk. And then Miss Molly broke her arm, and everything changed.

KRISSY: Molly's great with our Big Buckaroos, but she's also a barrel racer, which is a bit of a liability. She's usually flawless, but she was working with a new, young horse who took the third barrel turn a bit too fast and started to slide trip. Molly came right off. She was lucky the horse didn't crush her; she just landed funny. But I knew Molly couldn't handle those Big Buckaroos with only one arm. Luckily, my nephew was able to come in from Waco and help out.

> *Editor's Note: Barrel racing is a rodeo sport in which you ride a horse around a bunch of barrels as fast as you possibly can, for no apparent reason except that it sounds like a great way to break your neck.*

DAD: I had thought we were safe. But it never occurred to me that something might happen that would prevent Miss Molly from finishing out the summer with the Big Buckaroos. I let my guard down—I only walked Avery to Big Buckaroos on the first day when I met Miss Molly. I never should have assumed things would stay the same. So I blithely continued on, identifying cacti and painting sunsets like an imbecile, completely unaware that Avery had started a new relationship with someone I didn't even know existed.

AVERY: His name was Jackson, and he was a cowboy. A legit, walking, talking, roping, riding, desert-air-breathing, dusty cowboy.

JACKSON VALDEZ, *legit cowboy, rising junior at Baylor University*: When Aunt Krissy asked me to take over Big Buckaroos, I wasn't thrilled. I'd already been asked to leave Little Buckaroos last summer for not being sympathetic enough when one of the Buckaroos took a tumble off of his pony. Figured I was better off away from Little Lazy River. But then Aunt Krissy offered to almost double what I was making busing tables, and I agreed. Sure got a surprise when I saw the biggest Buckaroo.

AVERY: It was like something out of a movie. The door to the Big Buckaroos cabin blew open, and in came a tumbleweed. Then a man, silhouetted by the rising sun. His jeans and boots were perfectly worn, and the faint coat of dust only added to his allure. He looked up at me from under the brim of his cowboy hat, and our eyes met.

HUTCH: I had heard the story of Avery and the Cowboy when we came back to school junior year. I didn't think most of it was true then, and I don't think most of it is true now.

COCO: Avery's dad had taken away her phone. But the next postcard I got said *"SEXY COWBOY!!!!!"* on the flip side of the picture of a baby wearing a cowboy hat, so I knew things had taken a turn for the better.

HUTCH: Do I believe that Avery dated some guy named Jackson who liked horses? Yes. Do I believe he was preceded by tumbleweeds everywhere he went? No. No, I do not.

JACKSON: I'd been expecting the usual bunch of whining, sniffling toddlers, complaining about the heat and the horses being mean. Instead, I saw a blond angel in denim.

AVERY: He called me darlin'. Seriously. "What's your name, darlin'?" was the first thing he ever said. I had resigned myself to a summer free from boys, and then he appeared! Not just a boy, but a *cowboy*! It's not like I had a lot of competition, being surrounded by tweens, but I was still nervous. I couldn't blow my one chance. Luckily, he seemed just as happy to see me as I was to see him.

JACKSON: Big Buckaroos always do the first ride of the day early in the morning, after breakfast, before it gets too hot. I got all the kids on their horses, but once I saw that Avery had been riding Li'l Chunk, I asked if she'd rather try a real horse.

AVERY: What I honestly wanted was to ride on the horse with Jackson, like we were in a movie. But that seemed forward and also codependent. So I bid adieu to Li'l Chunk, and Jackson lifted me up and onto the saddle of a beautiful horse. We rode off into the desert next to each other, trailed by a dozen little kids who were only kind of ruining the moment.

JACKSON: Riding double on a horse isn't recommended. Not good for the horse. But I liked riding next to Avery anyway. Her seat wasn't half-bad for someone who'd just started. And her *seat* wasn't half-bad either, if you know what I mean.
  Editor's Note: Ewwwww, WHAT?!? I did not remember him being kind of gross and cheesy like this!!! I think I was blinded by his scruff.

HUTCH: That seat comment was the last straw. Time to wrap up this one and move on to the next.

AVERY: Jackson and I spent the summer horseback riding next to each other and holding hands and making out, and even though I never, ever stopped sweating, it was still pretty magical. We broke up because I went back to school, because duh. It was just a summer thing.

HUTCH: I feel like "just a summer thing" could have described a lot of AD's relationships—and not just the ones that took place in the summer. Maybe all of AD's relationships had ended because she was never fully *in* them, not with her whole self. Excuse me if I sound corny, but she never put all of her heart in them.

AVERY: I think Hutch had inadvertently stumbled across the reason my relationships didn't last—because my heart wasn't in them. I was a frosty, unlovable ice queen, incapable of love. I should just build a giant snowman and lock myself in an ice castle and let Coco go off and marry Kristoff.

HUTCH: I've gotten to know AD pretty well over the past four years, and she has a remarkable capacity for love. It's obvious in everything she does, from the way she treats her friends and talks about her parents and even takes care of that cat of hers. AD's relationships didn't end because she can't love—that's ridiculous. They ended because she simply hadn't found the right person. The statistical probability of finding your soul mate, if that's a concept you believe in, is so infinitesimally low it should be called a statistical improbability. The odds of that soul mate being someone you met in middle school, or high school, are lower still. Maybe we'd been asking ourselves the wrong question. It seemed like it would have been far more unusual if one of AD's relationships *had* lasted through the prom.

Editor's Note: "A remarkable capacity for love"?! I . . . oh, Hutch.

DAD: Avery introduced us to Jackson on our final night at Little Lazy River, during which there was a big formal farewell dinner in the mess hall. Was I surprised? Of course! She'd been dating this kid for two months and I'd never even seen him before. I had been well and truly bamboozled. But Avery had finished her whole summer reading list *and* booked herself on three college tours back home in California, so there was really nothing I could complain about. I resigned myself to the fact that Avery's social calendar would continue on as the paragon of insanity it had always been. I guess boys hadn't been the distraction I thought they were. If anything's distracting, it's all those apps. The only form of social media I endorse is LinkedIn. Everything else is superfluous nonsense.

HUTCH: AD's summer spree of vacation boyfriends in cinematic destinations continued. Maybe this section could be looked at as a deprivation experiment. In a dating desert, AD chose the only available option. Who was surprised? No one. She's like one of those plants that grows up through even the tiniest crack in the sidewalk. The will to date is strong in this one. Or *was* strong, I guess, since AD was done with dating. I still couldn't quite believe it. Well, I believed it, since I'd never known AD to back down from *anything* she'd set her mind to, but why, of all the times to be done with dating, did she have to pick right now?

Editor's Note: ??? I had no idea why Hutch had an opinion on the timing of my ban on boys, but when I asked him, he got defensive and said, "If you're really serious about this project, shouldn't you be creating a bar graph right now?" and then that turned into a whole thing because this project in no way lends itself to a bar graph and then I forgot what we were talking about.

JAKE DOE

COCO: When Avery busts a slump, she busts it hard. First, there was the cowboy. Then, there was the movie star. After sophomore year's epic fail, junior year was like Avery's equivalent of 1961—well, if JFK had only established the Peace Corps and not gotten embroiled in the Bay of Pigs.

BIZZY STANHOPE: I think reports of Jake Doe's "celebrity" have been wildly exaggerated. Jake Doe is not a movie star. He's on a TV show that's not even that popular. Or good. Like I guess some people know who he is, but most people would probably be like, "Jake who?"

NATALIE WAGNER, *random freshman*, Skyward *superfan*: OMG, *Skyward* is my favorite, favorite, favorite show of all time. It is literally the best thing on television. I never, *ever* miss an episode.

HUTCH: Would I classify *Skyward* as science fiction? Maybe in the very broadest sense of the term. But only if I had to. If someone was pointing a phaser at me.

MICHAEL FEELEY, *definitely not a* Skyward *fan*: Oh, sure, I know someone who actually watches *Skyward*. Liam is obsessed with it. It's mortifying. That's a show for twelve-year-old girls.

LIAM PADALECKI, *definitely a closet* Skyward *fan*: Oh, man, I don't watch that much *Skyward*! I watched it like one time. But I don't think it's fair that Michael and Hutch and Alex always judge it based solely on the admittedly limited merit of the pilot. Name one show that had a good pilot. Well, except you can't say *Firefly*. But that doesn't count, because that show is perfect. And also Fox didn't air the episodes in order, so who can really say what the pilot was?

> *Editor's Note: Hutch felt very strongly that I clarify that "Serenity" is the pilot episode of* Firefly, *and it's actually kind of hard to follow because it drops you into the universe without explaining very much. So although it is vastly enjoyable when rewatching, and gives us our first great Wash moment, whatever that means, it is by no means a perfect*

pilot. You're welcome for this extremely necessary tangent,
Ms. Segerson. I'm sure you really needed to know this.

NATALIE: *Skyward* takes place in a postapocalyptic dystopic future world where the government controls everything we do. Except there is one boy who will not be controlled. Nobody knows where he came from—he just fell out of the sky totally naked one day, covered in tattoos of numbers that no one knows what they mean. His name is Sky, and he will bring down the government by any means necessary—even if he has to break his own heart to do it. Because he fell in love with the daughter of the government leader. That part's important, too.

LIAM: I mean, there is no comparison between season one and season two. Season two is infinitely better. It's like watching two different shows! And those guys still won't give it a chance. Plus, Emma Rajpur, who plays the love interest, is insanely hot. And a total boss. I saw her speak on a panel at Comic-Con last year and every answer had the crowd on its feet.

Editor's Note: Here is where I had my wonderful, brilliant, amazing, beautiful idea that I thought might go toward erasing some of my karmic debt from being such a jerk to Liam in sixth grade.

HUTCH: *Skyward* is what would happen if someone put a bunch of different novels, movies, and TV shows in a blender and repackaged whatever got spit out with the new teen beat flavor of the month. It's hard to believe it's been on the air for four years. You'd think Sky would have taken down the government by now. Guess he's not quite the alien superspy everyone thinks he is.

NATALIE: But the best, best, best part about *Skyward* is Jake Doe. Jake plays Sky, and he is so incredibly crazy hot it's almost unbelievable. I have a poster of him taped up in my locker. I've had a poster of him taped up in my locker every year since the show premiered. I was only in middle school when Avery dated Jake Doe, but I still saw him. I saw him pick her up after school one day, and he's actually even hotter in person, if you can believe it. Shorter than I thought he'd be, but hotter, too.

COCO: I don't want you to go into this thinking that Avery stalked Jake Doe or anything like that. No, the way she met him was pure dumb luck. Well, the locations manager for *Skwyard*, and pure dumb luck.

JAKE DOE, *semi-famous TV actor, ex-boyfriend*: Our locations manager had this super-specific vision for when Sky's memories are implanted with a false vision of an alternate life of privilege in a society much closer to our current, present-day one, where he's just a typical teenager. Basically, they wanted to find a fancy private school, but for whatever reason, none of the million private schools in LA were good enough. At the time, I was whining like crazy about having to drive out to San Anselmo, but it turned out to be totally worth it.

COCO: Nobody knew *Skyward* was filming at our school. I guess the administration was worried that whatever *Skyward* superfans went to San Anselmo would swarm the set and throw their panties at Jake Doe or whatever.

NATALIE: I think it was the meanest thing ever that the school didn't tell us *Skyward* was filming there. It would have been a dream come true to see Jake Doe bring *Skyward* to life! I've never forgiven Principal Patel for keeping all of us from that, and I never will.

PRINCIPAL PATEL: Normally, I wouldn't condone use of school grounds as a film set, but the *Skyward* producers offered a very generous contribution toward the capital campaign for the new performing arts center. Fortunately, as they were equally concerned with keeping Jake Doe's whereabouts private, it was relatively easy to keep the entire situation quiet. Well, until Avery Dennis started dating Jake Doe. Has the school been used as a location since? Oh, absolutely not. Yet another addendum to the handbook we owe to Avery Dennis. I prefer my students to be in the news only for academic achievements.

JAKE: We were filming on a Saturday, so the school was pretty empty. It was supposed to be an alternate reality, except they wanted the hallways to look abandoned? I don't know, man, sometimes I don't understand these scripts either. I was leaning against the building by the track, looking out dramatically into the middle distance, which is something Sky does a lot on the show. All of a sudden, this blond blur came sprinting out of nowhere, running full tilt at me.

AVERY: It was the first weekend of the school year, and I *had* to get into that building.

JAKE: I thought it was a stalker. I've never had anything too scary happen, but a girl went after my face with a Sharpie once. Wanted to mark me as hers. But I heard one of the guys on *Adam's Fall* had a similar incident, except with a razor. A female fan didn't like that he grew a beard for season two, and she decided to try to take matters into her own hands. So it could have been a lot worse.

> *Editor's Note:* Adam's Fall *is a drama about a young single father living in the remote Alaskan wilderness, and the sexy lady helicopter pilot he may or may not be in love with. It's probably worse than* Skyward.

AVERY: We had a lab report due on Monday, and I'd left my notes in my locker. I knew Hutch would *kill* me if my section of the lab was subpar, or God forbid, missing altogether.

HUTCH: The first lab report of the school year is absolutely crucial. It introduces your scientific style to the teacher, and also establishes your place in the class order. I didn't want to just finish out the year the best. I wanted to start off the year as the best. The first lab report of the year is your scientific calling card, and I always want mine to be flawless.

CRESSIDA SCHROBENHAUSER-CLONAN: The worst kind of scientist is a careless one, and that sorry description fits Avery perfectly. Can you imagine if she hadn't been able to use her dubious charms to flirt her way into the school? Everyone knows the first lab report of the year is the most important one. If her part of the lab had been missing, Hutch would have had every right to drop her like a molten ball of tungsten. If only.

AVERY: I didn't have a plan, exactly. Well, my plan was to drive to school, and then get into the building by any means necessary. While I was bored during PE that week, I'd noticed a window in the gym whose latch looked a little weak. So I guess my plan was to climb the wall like Spider-Man, jimmy open the window, slide on in through it, and drop to the floor with the grace and agility of a cat. I think, even at the time, I realized this plan was most likely impossible, so when a Plan B appeared, I obviously sprinted right at it.

JAKE: I saw Avery first, because I was staring dramatically off into the middle distance, like I said. But before I could get too nervous, I realized she wasn't coming for me at all. She sprinted right toward one of the crew guys.

AVERY: I ran toward the person who had the largest visible key ring—he had a ton of keys clipped onto his belt with one of those carabiner things. I thought he'd be the most likely person to let me into the building.

JAKE: It was immediately obvious that she wasn't interested in me, or *Skyward*, or the shoot, or any of it. How did I know? I could hear everything—something about a lab report and needing to get into the building, like, now. Totally ruined the take. Director was pissed, but I thought it was hilarious.

AVERY: The guy with the keys wasn't going to let me in. I couldn't believe it! So close, and yet so far. He was trying to escort me off the school grounds, when salvation intervened in the hottest of forms.

JAKE: We were taking five because the shot was ruined anyway, so I came over to see what was happening. Taylor wasn't going to let her in, but he did when I asked him to.

AVERY: At first I was so relieved I was getting my notes that it didn't register exactly who the blindingly hot guy walking me to my locker was.

JAKE: Avery was cool, man. She didn't get all weird around me, or act like she was trying too hard to *not* be weird, which is worse, in some ways. She actually spent most of our walk to her locker talking about her lab partner, of all the random things.

AVERY: It was right when I closed my locker and locked eyes with Jake's famous hazel gaze that I knew who he was. I'd seen him brooding at me on my TV the exact way he was brooding at me then, in real life!

HUTCH: I don't understand how Avery could have run right past an entire television crew—lights, camera, everything—and not have realized who she was with. I guess it's flattering, kind of—I'd scared her so badly about turning in poor science homework it superseded any rational powers of observation. Good to know she had her priorities in line.

JAKE: I hadn't dated anyone my manager hadn't set me up with since *Skyward* came out. I couldn't even remember the last time I'd been around someone my age who wasn't in the industry. Listening to Avery talk about science homework and lab partners and cheeseburgers just felt . . . normal. It felt *good*. And she was prettier without makeup than the last pop star my manager insisted I take out was with fifteen pounds of foundation caked on. Avery was real, man.

AVERY: When Jake Doe asked me if I wanted to get a milk shake, I thought I'd heard him wrong.

JAKE: We bagged the shoot for the day, and I had my driver take us to In-N-Out. I was hoping no one would bother us since not many people knew we were filming in San Anselmo. And nobody did bother us . . . then.

COCO: "Jake grabs shake with mystery blond!" That was the first headline. Tamsin Brewer, of all people, FB-messaged it to me. That blond was no mystery to me. I didn't know anyone else who looked that happy with an In-N-Out shake. I started texting Avery immediately, but she didn't respond for the longest time. Probably because she was busy gazing into those dreamy, famous hazel eyes.

JAKE: I didn't know the paps had spotted us then. I just knew that I hadn't laughed so much in the past year as I did in the hour getting a burger with Avery, that turned into two hours, that turned into three, that turned into her getting five missed calls from her mom and me having to apologize profusely to her parents when my driver dropped her off.

PAUL DENNIS aka DAD, *father, not a fan of* Skyward: The following day, Jake—or whoever his publicity people are—sent us a huge basket filled with *Skyward* promotional materials. I have no idea why on God's green earth that boy thought we would enjoy those.

COCO: And that's how Avery became a celebrity girlfriend. She was the talk of San Anselmo Prep on Monday morning— Tamsin really spread that "Jake Grabs Shake" article around the school.

BIZZY: Avery was *so* obnoxious when she started dating Jake Doe. She, like, wouldn't talk about it at all, like it was some kind of state secret. Not that I cared, or whatever, because I could not have been less interested in whatever happened on her stupid date with that Z-list "celebrity," but the way she was being so secretive about it was beyond annoying.

AVERY: Of course I was excited that I'd gone out with Jake Doe. I mean, it was Jake Doe, for Pete's sake! But I didn't want to talk about it with anyone but Coco. Even just from that first day with Jake, I could tell his privacy was really important to him. I didn't want to betray that. And I got the feeling from him that he wanted to be as normal as possible, even though there was nothing normal about him. But everyone was being a complete freak about it. Well, everyone except Coco and Hutch.

HUTCH: Oh, yeah, sure, I was pumped about the lab report and the A I knew we'd get—and did—but everything else about that Monday pretty much sucked. I couldn't even compete with the Robby Monroes and Tripp Gomez-Parkers of the world, and now AD was dating a movie star? I mean, not that I was competing with them. I just mean that no normal guy had a chance. I mean, not that I wanted a chance, it was just a, uh, observation.

> *Editor's Note: Compete?! Chance?! What?! Hutch was normally so lucid, and now I could barely understand him at all. I wanted to understand him, but I was worried I was reading too much into it—I mean, not that I was trying to read anything into it. I mean—oh, forget it.*

COCO: Avery was "Mystery Blond" on Monday. But by the next weekend, she was "Jake Doe's Girlfriend, Avery Dennis." The press kept calling it a Cinderella story—movie star sweeps normal high school girl off her feet!—and suddenly, Jake was everywhere. Which meant Avery was everywhere, too. And there is nothing weirder than seeing your best friend on a gossip website.

BIZZY: I think the most memorable thing about Avery's first paparazzi pics was that her pores were so enormous I could see them individually. If I knew someone was going to be taking pictures of me, I would at least *attempt* to fix my face.

> *Editor's Note: Mean!!! I didn't know someone was going to take my picture! That's the whole point of paparazzi! I had thought I was going to Starbucks with my boyfriend for an iced passion tea. Do I wish I hadn't worn sweatpants? Absolutely. But I refuse to waste a moment of brain space feeling regret over my pores, which Coco assured me were not visible in the slightest.*

COCO: Sure, it seemed like the Avery and Jake thing came out of nowhere, but *all* of Avery's relationships had always gone from zero to sixty in like three seconds flat! It was just more visible at this point. Besides, they were basically long distance, and that always forces a fast commitment. LA is practically in a different state from San Anselmo.

> *Editor's Note: On a nonstop flight, it's only an hour and ten minutes. There are perks to dating a celebrity! Even if the drawback is you usually only see him on the weekends, and only in San Anselmo instead of glamorous LA, because your*

parents are remarkably lame about supporting a sweet jet-setting lifestyle.

JAKE: My manager was pissed that I'd basically dropped off the premieres and parties circuit, but I loved going to visit Avery in San Anselmo. And the whole stupid Movie Star Dates All-American Girl angle was getting a ton of press, so my manager wasn't *that* pissed.

COCO: I think the weirdest thing about Avery's relationship with Jake was how *normal* it was. Mostly, he came to visit us here, because her parents wouldn't let her fly down to LA to see him unsupervised. They spent most of their time hanging out at Avery's house, or hanging out with me and Alfie—my boyfriend at the time—at his house. Basically places no one would take Jake's picture. They'd cruise through the In-N-Out drive-through and roll up at Alfie's house with bags full of food, and we'd play video games or Ping-Pong. That's probably the thing I remember the most about Jake—he was surprisingly lethal at Ping-Pong. He and Alfie would get into these, like, hourlong volleys, and then get pissed when Avery finished all the fries. But if you're dating Avery, you should know that she considers letting French fries get cold a capital offense.

Editor's Note: I feel like this history should have devoted more time to the fact that Coco dated a guy name Alfie for a really, really long time.

JAKE: Those were some of the most fun weeks of my life. I felt like I was finally having the normal teenage experience I'd missed out on. I even got to go to a homecoming dance!

BIZZY: Oh my God, everyone was being a total freak about Jake Doe at homecoming. Even the teachers kept taking pictures with him, which confirmed every suspicion I ever had about how sad their lives were. He even got crowned Homecoming King. He doesn't even go here!

Editor's Note: Bizzy was so pissed. So was Meghan Gossner, because she'd thought she had Homecoming Queen in the bag, then I won somehow—well, I know how, because I was there with Jake—and juniors weren't supposed to win at all. But it kind of sucked, because I spent the whole night sitting around while Jake politely took selfies with every single person who went to my school—and yes, some of the teachers, too. But not all of them. Thank you for being cool, Ms. Segerson. The most important part of this story, though, is that Coco was our Homecoming Queen this year, so Bizzy never got that tiara plopped onto her ratty blond head. Hahaha! This is probably why she's so bonkers about Prom Queen.

COCO: Avery and Jake really only dated for a couple weeks. Although I wonder how long it actually was in real time, since they usually only saw each other once or twice a week. When you put it all together, maybe they only dated each other for a couple hours?

JAKE: We'd have dinner with her parents after school sometimes, then hang out with her friends, just doing, like, nothing . . . it was totally normcore, man.

AVERY: See, I feel like junior year everyone thought I was dating Jake because of his glamorous lifestyle. But I couldn't shake the feeling that maybe Jake was dating *me* because of my not-so-glamorous lifestyle. I wondered if he liked the fact that I was "normal" more than he actually liked me.

COCO: The official story—the one that broke on San Anselmo Prep's campus and *TMZ* simultaneously—was that Avery and Jake parted ways due to the pressures of his lifestyle. That she just wanted to be a normal teen and was tired of the paparazzi. Although, honestly, they like never bothered us unless Jake was there, and Jake was a total·hermit most of the time he was here.

JAKE: Listen, man, I have no hard feelings toward Avery. It's weird, the way I live—and I know that—and it probably wasn't fair to her to have a boyfriend who lived five hours away and had to go to a certain number of parties and premieres her parents wouldn't let her go to. I was sad when she dumped me, but I'd known my sweet suburban escape couldn't last forever. Besides, my manager said the Avery angle had kind of played out at that point, and it was a good time to date someone more high profile.

Editor's Note: He started dating the country singer Camryn Sweets pretty soon after we broke up, and in the next couple months, she had her first crossover pop hit with the single "Blonder Than Her." Coco swears it's about me, but I'm not convinced.

BIZZY: I didn't believe any of that garbage the Internet was spinning about Jake and Avery's split being mutual, and I don't think anybody else did, either. It was obvious he'd dumped her—just look at how fast he started dating Camryn Sweets! I was pretty sure Jake Doe's whole relationship with Avery had been some kind of poorly planned publicity stunt that had gone on for far too long. His management team was obviously terrible; otherwise, he wouldn't have been on *Skyward.*

COCO: I don't know how to say this without it sounding creepy—but I'll try. In some ways, I feel like Jake Doe was the first of Avery's boyfriends who could actually match the force of her personality. He is beyond charismatic. I think, if we're trying to mine these old relationships for subtext, that's what I see here. Jake was confident enough to stand on his own, driven enough to keep up with Avery, and also let her do her own thing. Jake came to her tennis matches, even if it did cause a lot of problems with all of the moms trying to take pictures with him. Overall, Jake was probably one of Avery's *best* boyfriends. And maybe he'd matured enough now that he'd be less obsessed with being a normal high schooler and more obsessed with just being Avery's boyfriend. I wondered if he was single—I'd seen online that he'd been spotted out to dinner with Emmanuelle Oliveira, from *Adam's Fall*, but that was just dinner. And who knew if that was real or just a publicity thing anyway—they were on the same network, after all. Maybe this would be a chance for Avery and Jake to rekindle things! Yes, I know Avery's sworn off dating, but there's gotta be some kind of movie star ex-boyfriend exception clause to that kind of thing, right?

Editor's Note: There is absolutely not. I am D-O-N-E done with dating until we finish this. I don't care if Jake Doe is available.

HUTCH: I know Avery had said she was going to prom on her own, but part of me was waiting for Avery to ask Jake Doe to the prom. It would be hard to resist a celebrity, right? Seems like that's the kind of guy who would make anyone break a no-dating vow. He's professionally handsome, after all. That is literally his job.

Editor's Note: If I was going to break my no-dating vow for anyone, it certainly wouldn't be Jake Doe . . .

COCO: I didn't think it would *hurt* to ask Jake about the prom. We already knew he looked great in a tux, from that time he had to go to a black-tie ball at the Supreme Leader's Mansion in order to stop an assassination attempt from a misguided group of rebel space banditos, because even though Jake was *also* trying to take down the government, the rebels had to be stopped, for some reason that I can't remember.

HUTCH: AD *did* ask someone about prom, but not the person I thought she was going to ask.

JAKE: It was pretty weird when Avery asked me if Emma was free on Friday—they weren't exactly friends. I know Emma was supposed to go to some new bottled-water launch, but she'd probably skip it if I asked.

HUTCH: It took Jake a while to figure out what AD was asking—I think he's kind of slow—but I knew what she was doing immediately.

JAKE: But then again, I wasn't that surprised when Avery asked if I thought Emma would go to her prom. Everyone's in love with Emma. Even my ex-girlfriends, apparently.

HUTCH: I had never seen anything like this. I had never felt— uh, I mean, I'd seen AD do a lot of cool things these past four years, but this might have taken the cake.

AVERY: I'd gotten to know Hutch's friends since I started this project, and even though they may have said they didn't want to go to prom, I realized that *I* wanted them to go to prom. I liked them, and I wanted to spend time with them, but more importantly, they were part of our senior class, and I wanted us all to experience this final high school rite of passage together. Besides, I knew once I got them there, they'd have fun. And I'd have fun hanging out with them, too.

HUTCH: AD got Emma Rajpur—*Emma Rajpur!*—to agree to go to the prom with my best friend, perpetually single Liam Padalecki. This was proof that miracles happened.

AVERY: Jake put me on the phone with Emma Rajpur's manager and I lined up the whole thing—apparently, bottled water is bad for her brand now anyway, because we're all supposed to be using glass water bottles. Plus, "celebrities going to prom with regular people" is still really hot right now, even though it's played out to ask on Twitter.

HUTCH: No, of course I wasn't mad Liam was going to prom! I would never stand between Liam and his dream girl. She is literally his dream girl—Liam has a poster of Emma Rajpur on his ceiling. Of course I wanted him to go to prom with her. Sure, Ultimate Game Night would get pushed back a little bit, but Michael and Alex and I could play some more casual three-player games until Liam came over. Who knows, maybe Emma would come after prom, too. She might be secretly into RPG. She's been at Comic-Con for the last few years, after all. She might have picked up a thing or two.

AVERY: The whole thing was going to be an amazing surprise. All Hutch had to do was make sure Liam got into a tux—which Coco and I would rent from somewhere—then a limo would pull up with Emma Rajpur inside. I couldn't wait to film it and then remix it to an inspirational mash-up that included the

Skyward opening theme. See, *this* is what prom is about—dreams coming true! Not some stupid plastic tiara.

COCO: Oh, we'd get the tux all right—and maybe fit in a small makeover. Liam's honestly not, uh, *bad*-looking . . . but his hair could use a bit of an update.

HUTCH: So Emma Rajpur was coming to the prom. And Avery hadn't asked Jake to go with her, which meant she must have been *really* committed to this whole no-dating thing, which was just kind of . . . well. It was what it was.

Editor's Note: Jake had nothing to do with "this whole no-dating thing." I didn't want to go to prom with Jake. But there was someone I thought I might want to . . . No, never mind. I made a decision and I'm sticking to it.

NILS HENDQVIST

COACH KELLY, *tennis coach at San Anselmo Prep*: There are no official rules that expressly prohibit romantic relationships between athletic teammates at San Anselmo Prep. I know this because I've spent the past year trying my hardest to institute that exact rule.

PRINCIPAL PATEL, *principal of San Anselmo Prep*: No, I have absolutely no plans to attempt to place restrictions upon students' dating lives through rules in the student handbook. Are you kidding? Do you have any idea how many parents at this school are lawyers? Wait—don't put that part in.

COACH KELLY: When Avery Dennis asked out Nils Hendqvist, it almost ended my teaching career.

> *Editor's Note: I had no idea I had inflicted such turmoil. I really should have stepped up my game during Teacher Appreciation Week. At the very least, I should have gotten Coach Kelly a Starbucks gift card or something.*

COCO: Nils is a very, like, compact guy, I guess you would say? He's barely taller than Avery and almost as blond as she is.

HUTCH: Once again, AD was dating an athlete. Most might assume an obsession with physical fitness—the search for the prototypical "hot bod," if you will—but I knew AD better than that. No, this was about something that lurked far beneath a toned rectus abdominis muscle. This was about AD's insane competitive drive and lust for winning. Naturally, she'd be drawn to other competitive maniacs.

Editor's Note: Hutch was at it again with the air quotes. Also the phrase "hot bod" coming out of Hutch's mouth was moderately disturbing.

NILS HENDQVIST, *ex-boyfriend and nationally ranked teen tennis player*: Avery is a decent player, but she tends to let her emotions get the best of her. It is the biggest fault in her game.

COACH KELLY: Basically, with Dennis and Hendqvist, you see two opposing styles of play. Two different schools of thought on the game of tennis. Hendqvist is all control and precision. Dennis is all power and passion. When they started dating, it was like a lava flow met an avalanche, but instead of tempering each other, they exploded into an icy, fiery apocalypse.

NILS: Oh, you wanted to talk about the time I *dated* Avery? It hardly signified.

Editor's Note: It hardly signified?!?! Ouch.

COCO: I don't even know how to measure how long they dated, since they broke up and got back together again like a billion times. We call it the Nils Debacle for a reason. The whole thing was a mess.

NILS: I do remember how irrational she was. I would attempt to give her pointers on the weak areas of her game—her drop shots, for example—and she would react like an insane person. Constructive criticism is essential to improvement.

AVERY: Nothing about Nils's tennis "pointers" was constructive. He would just harangue me for my weak playing. Like he was so much better than me, which he absolutely *is not*. It was the worst.

COCO: They were always fighting, then Avery would dump him, but she'd ask him out again by the end of the day. Although Nils never reacted to any of it. He would look at her in this totally cool, level way and say nothing. Actually, because of all of Nils's non-reactions, in some ways it was more like Avery was fighting with herself.

AVERY: Fighting with Nils was like fighting with a brick wall. It was maddening. He never responded. Which just made me madder and madder.

NILS: All of Avery's faults are the same on the tennis court as in life. She cannot act from a place of logic. She cannot detach from a situation. She cannot converse rationally. She can only operate from emotion, invest too much, and scream. That is all.

HUTCH: I didn't know what Nils was talking about. AD is an extremely logical person. Clearly, Nils had never conducted an experiment with her. Is she emotional? Sure. Can she be a bit dramatic sometimes? Yeah, maybe. But that's only because she *cares* so much. She invests herself 110 percent in everything she does. And what's so wrong with being emotional anyway? The greatest scientific discoveries in history have been spurred by passion *and* reason, in equal measures. And that's AD exactly.
   *Editor's Note: Wow, Hutch really *has my back.**

COCO: I don't know if I'd say there was any kind of fallout from them breaking up, because the whole time they were dating, it was kind of like they were breaking up, you know?

COACH KELLY: Oh, sure, I remember when they broke up. It was right around the end of the season. Dozens of tennis balls disappeared. No confirmation, but I'm pretty sure Dennis had something to do with it.

COCO: Oh my God, how had I almost forgotten about the tennis balls?! When Avery reminded me about them, *then* I remembered why we called this the Nils Debacle.

HUTCH: I was on my way to English in a very crowded hallway when Nils opened his locker. Dozens and dozens of tennis balls spilled out, bouncing merrily down the hallway. It was total chaos. You'd be surprised how many tennis balls can fit in a locker. And how many freshman girls think screaming is an appropriate response to a hallway full of tennis balls. Were they scary? I still don't get it.

NILS: No, Avery's stunts did not amuse me. Nor upset me overmuch. A locker full of tennis balls? A testament to her juvenile nature.
    Editor's Note: If I was responsible for the tennis balls, which I'm not saying I am, I would be completely insulted.

PRINCIPAL PATEL: There was no proof whatsoever that Avery Dennis was responsible for the incident with the tennis balls. I was positive it was her, and yet, with no proof and no confession, there was nothing I could do. Avery Dennis does not crack under any amount of questioning.

NILS: Once our romantic relationship ended, we returned to an amicable working relationship as teammates, nothing more. We have been playing for San Anselmo Prep together since that time without incident.

AVERY: At least I knew exactly why I dumped Nils. He was a cold Swedish fish.

COCO: Swedish fish. That's what she always called him when they were fighting last year. And I'd be all, "Avery, how would you feel if someone called me a Korean gochujang?" but she did not understand the analogy I was making.

NILS: The Swedish Fish in America are not even anything like the Pastellfiskar in Sweden! And Sweden has much better candies! Pastellfiskar is one of our *worst* candies, honestly!

Editor's Note: Nils was more passionate about Swedish candy than he was about me. I think that tells you everything you need to know.

HUTCH: So AD and Nils were alike in some ways—competitive drive, love of tennis, etc.—but too different in their approach to relationships. What we had here were two fundamentally different temperaments.

AVERY: I really hope I don't bump into Nils at prom. He would probably spend the whole time critiquing my dance moves and talking about how emotional I am.

HUTCH: There was a lesson here, though, if AD could see it—it doesn't really matter if two people share surface interests. That's not what makes a good couple. The things they need to have in common are far more fundamental.

Editor's Note: No duh, Hutch. Almost-done-with-high-school Avery has learned at least that much.

COACH KELLY: When Dennis explained why she was asking all these questions and doing this interview, the first thing I did was beg her not to get back together with Hendqvist. The tennis season may have been over, but the two of them could manage to give me an ulcer from afar.

AVERY: I reassured Coach Kelly that was definitely not happening.

COACH KELLY: It's an interesting idea, revisiting the past. But it's just like tennis, really—you may play the same opponent again and again, but they're never *really* the same. You come to the court different each time. Your opponent comes to the court different each time. That's why the *game* is different each time. No matter how similar the circumstances may seem, you can't go back. There is no way to re-create a game.

Editor's Note: I felt like this was probably really wise, but when you've played as many tennis matches as I have, you really start to hate sports analogies.

HUTCH: A subtle shift had happened somewhere along the way, and I wasn't sure where it had occurred. AD seemed less into her boyfriends. Sure, she had spoken of Jake Doe fondly, but she didn't seem quite as obsessed as she had with her earlier romantic encounters. Why the change, though? That was the real question.

Editor's Note: I had a hypothesis, but I sure wasn't going to share it with Hutch. I was starting to wonder if everyone I had dated over the past couple years had just been a place-holder for the person I really wanted but didn't know I really wanted, until it was way too late. It takes a real genius to figure out she has feelings for someone the last week of school after sitting next to him for four years.

COCO: We had now interviewed all of Avery's ex-boyfriends but one, and if we'd learned anything, it was that maybe Avery *should* stay single. Not all of them were horrible, but I didn't think any of them really *got* Avery. Not completely, anyway.

HUTCH: All of these guys had remembered the wrong things about AD. Her long blond hair. How pretty she is. How popular she is. No one had spent enough time talking about how smart she is, how driven, how funny, how caring. How she can be kind of despotic, but you can't even get mad at her because she's almost always right, and the way she wanted to do things was probably better anyway. I was glad her hair was gone. I hoped people could now see the AD I see: a brilliant, bossy, beautiful genius. Maybe it was good she had given up dating since all these clowns had seen was her hair, even if it meant . . . well. I thought it meant she just hadn't found the right guy. But if AD thought it meant she was done with dating, I knew she was done. Don't try to argue with her. You'll lose.

AVERY: I was almost done interviewing all of my exes, and all I felt was confused. I now knew why all of my relationships had ended. But I barely knew why most of them had even started! And I certainly didn't know what any of those relationships said about me. Worst of all, I was starting to wonder if this whole "no dating thing" had been a colossal mistake. Because all of those things Hutch had said about me made me think that maybe the ban on boyfriends *wasn't* the solution I'd been looking for after all. Well, maybe interviewing Luke Murphy would bring me some brilliant insight and answer all of my questions. Before I called Luke, Hutch texted me that he had something to show me. It was the day before prom, and I was desperate to see what he'd pulled together. I drove over to meet him ASAP . . . only the address he'd sent me wasn't the B of A building at all. I drove to San Francisco as fast as I could to find Hutch.

HUTCH SAVES THE PROM

HUTCH: I realized from the very beginning my plan was kind of a Hail Mary. But I had one thing going for me: time. Not a lot of time, but enough. Bizzy Stanhope, in a classic Bond villain move, had told AD her entire evil plan before it unfolded. Logically, this made no sense. If Bizzy hadn't said anything about the prom, everyone would have shown up at the B of A building, discovered there was no prom, and chaos would have ensued. That would have been way more diabolical.

AVERY: Hutch didn't know Bizzy well enough to know that logic never comes into play. Besides, I knew she didn't *really* want prom to be canceled, because then how could she be Prom Queen? She just wanted it moved somewhere stupid that would make me look bad. So she gave me just enough time to fix it, but poorly. Holy cow. That's actually *super* diabolical. Maybe Bizzy Stanhope *is* a Bond villain.

HUTCH: AD said the original venue was a no-go, but I felt like I had no choice but to get someone from B of A on the phone and plead my case. It was worth a shot. I was banking on the hypothesis that Bizzy Stanhope was well known in her dad's office, and that whomever I spoke with would understand immediately why I needed to save the prom, and they'd hopefully be able to work some scheduling magic. My hypothesis was proven to be one hundred percent accurate.

KAREN NAKAYAMA, *Event Space Coordinator for the San Francisco branch of the Bank of America*: It took James several tries to get me on the phone—my assistant is terrific at weeding out unknown callers—but he was relentless. But once we finally spoke and he explained the situation, I understood immediately. All of Ted's children are famous here—especially Bizzy. This juvenile prom stunt sounds like a classic move from the Bizzy Stanhope playbook. One time she threw a burrito at one of our junior analysts.

    Editor's Note: I always forget that Hutch's name is really James. It took me way too long to figure out who she was talking about.

CRAIG LEAMAN, *junior analyst*: There was no burrito. Yes, the day after the alleged burrito incident, I departed for two weeks' paid vacation. Completely unrelated. Why do you ask?

KAREN: I had hoped I could help James out from the beginning—he was remarkably polite and articulate—*and* I had a feeling this was about that Avery girl he kept talking about. Now *that* really tugged at my heartstrings. Can you imagine? The only thing my high school boyfriend ever did for me was my Spanish homework.

HUTCH: I just told Ms. Nakayama that, uh, I needed a favor because the, uh, senior class had worked really hard this year, and, uh, prom was important to our experience. As a senior class. I wasn't doing this for a girl. Well, I was obviously doing it *for* AD, I just wasn't doing it because, well, because I thought anything would happen. She was done with guys, and when AD says she's done with something, she's done. I knew I had no shot. But that didn't matter. What mattered was saving the prom, because prom is important to AD. And AD is important to me.

KAREN: Unfortunately, there was absolutely nothing I could do. The space was booked, and as much as I wanted to help James out, I couldn't.

AVERY: On the one hand, I was sort of surprised when I pulled up in front of the California Academy of Sciences, but on the other hand, I wasn't surprised at all. Of course Hutch would solve any problem with science. But what kind of prom venue opportunities could a science academy possibly provide? I trusted Hutch, but I'm not gonna lie, I was nervous.

JUSTIN CASTILLEJO, *Director of Special Events and Volunteer Services at the California Academy of Sciences*: Hutch has been volunteering at the academy since he was in middle school. He's more valuable than half our employees. I speak for everyone on the staff when I say there's nothing we wouldn't do for Hutch. We would move heaven and earth if he asked. And when he asked, luckily, heaven—well, space—just happened to be free.

AVERY: Hutch was waiting for me outside, looking sort of un-Hutch-like in surprisingly cool sunglasses. I could tell he was nervous. He wiped his hands on his khakis a couple times as he led me through the building, stopping, eventually, in front of the doors to the Morrison Planetarium.

HUTCH: I was freaking out. I thought the room looked pretty good—really good—but AD's standards are crazy high in everything, and I knew her expectations would be off the charts for prom. I think I had a small cardiac episode as I pushed open the door to the planetarium.

AVERY: The first thing I saw was the night sky, a deep ink blue dotted with glittering stars. The whole ceiling of the planetarium was lit up so beautifully I could barely take my eyes off it—it felt like the stars were all around us. But that wasn't all. There were lampposts with glowing lights ringing the room and strings of twinkling lights hanging between them. There were paintings of shadowy café scenes and Paris at night propped up against the walls. Deep blue curtains covered the tables where refreshments would be, and Hutch had somehow made an illuminated Eiffel Tower, taller than me, for taking pictures in front of. The floor had been cleared of seats, so there was space for dancing, and there was a giant clock painted on the dance floor, hands set permanently at twelve o'clock. It was Midnight in Paris, the prom theme I'd been dreaming of since I was a freshman, come to life. It was more beautiful than I'd ever imagined it could be. And Hutch had done it for me.

HUTCH: She didn't say anything. For like seven minutes, she just didn't say anything. Not a single word. It was the longest I'd heard AD be silent on a day that didn't involve standardized testing. And then she said, in this quiet little voice that didn't sound anything like her, "Oh, Hutch."

AVERY: "Do you like it?" he asked, and he sounded so nervous, he almost didn't sound like the confident Hutch I knew at all.

HUTCH: "It's perfect," she said, and the way she looked at me, I felt like . . . I felt like . . . Well, I felt like I finally knew how Michael Faraday must have felt when he first produced an electric current by moving a wire through a magnetic field.

AVERY: How did he do it? How was it possible? I didn't understand. It was a miracle.

LIAM PADALECKI: I've pretty much run the San Anselmo Prep theater department's tech crew single-handedly for the past four years.

MICHAEL FEELEY: Liam said *what*? Single-handedly?! Oh, please! Everyone knows the theater lives or dies on the success of its light plot! Liam just fannies about with a paintbrush!

Editor's Note: I could not believe he used the phrase "fannies about."

HUTCH: It kind of *was* a miracle, honestly. It was a miracle that the planetarium was free, and that they were generous enough to donate their space to the San Anselmo Prep senior class for five hours on a Saturday night. And the theater department at school did *Gigi* last year, so we were insanely lucky that a lot of this stuff was buried in the prop room, ready to be stolen for the greater good of the San Anselmo Prep senior class. Michael hung the lights and wired the lamps. I did any necessary construction, and then Liam painted the art scattered around the walls. Oh, and Alex sewed all of the tablecloths.

ALEX MANEVITZ: I didn't sew anything, okay? I don't sew!
Editor's Note: He was lying. If Hutch said Alex sewed the tablecloth, then Alex sewed the tablecloth. Also I turned down a hallway at school once and saw him sewing ruffles on a dress the week before Hello, Dolly! *opened. So that boy for sure sews.*

AVERY: If Hutch had done all of this . . . for the prom . . . for *me*, maybe . . . then I had to ask. And maybe there were reasons that necessitated breaking a "no-boys ban." Like when someone gives you a room full of stars. That seemed like a pretty good reason to me. Because I was realizing that maybe what mattered wasn't whether you were in a relationship or not. What mattered was that you could still be yourself in that relationship. And I knew I could always be myself with Hutch, because Hutch knew who I really was. I could feel hope inflating in my chest like the beautiful midnight-blue balloons I would have ordered if I hadn't put Tamsin Brewer in charge of decorations.

HUTCH: She had been standing next to me the whole time, looking up at the stars. All of a sudden, I felt her hand reaching for mine. I took it, and our hands fit together perfectly, like we should have been holding hands for the past four years.

AVERY: Hutch has really nice hands. I've often admired them while he was dissecting a fetal pig or igniting the flame on the Bunsen burner. But he's even better at holding hands than he is at dissecting fetal pigs.

HUTCH: "Hey, Hutch?" she said.

AVERY: He said, "Yes, Avery?" Avery. Not AD.

HUTCH: She said, "Do you think you might go to prom?"

AVERY: And he said, "You know what? I think I just might."

HUTCH: Why did I change my mind? Because I wanted to go with Avery. I wanted to spend the last big night of high school with the person who was part of so many of my best memories of high school. Now that San Anselmo Prep was almost in my rearview mirror, I was surprised to find that I wanted one last big night to celebrate it and all the people who had made it what it was. Besides, only an idiot would turn down an opportunity to spend time at a planetarium after hours.

AVERY: The prom looked perfect. But I knew it could only *be* perfect if Hutch was there. And all of his friends. And even Cressida Schrobenhauser-Clonan and Bizzy Stanhope, God help us all. Because they were all part of our senior class, and they all should be part of our prom. Because I knew prom was going to be an experience, and I wanted it to be an experience I fell in love with—and I knew that would only be possible if Hutch was there. And now he was going, and I was pretty sure I could trick him into dancing. And yes, I had given up guys, but Hutch wasn't *just* a guy. He was Hutch. And that meant something.

Editor's Note: So I kissed him. ☺ ☺ ☺ ☺ ☺

LUKE MURPHY

HUTCH: I really, really didn't understand why we had to interview Luke Murphy.

AVERY: I told Hutch it was for continuity! And closure! And . . . and consequences!

> *Editor's Note: Hutch said, "What* consequences *are you anticipating?!" He seemed to think I'd do something to Luke Murphy involving a chair that would get me expelled the week before we graduated. As if! I could have a rational conversation with the miscreant who dumped me the week before prom.*

COCO: Oh, I got it. I totally got it. You still want to know *why* someone dumped you, even if there's not a snowball's chance in San Anselmo of you getting back together with that person. Besides, Luke was Tripp's best friend, and it would be great if things weren't awkward at the prom. It was time to get some closure up in this piece.

> *Editor's Note: "Up in this piece"?! She had been spending way too much time with Tripp.*

LUKE MURPHY, *ex-boyfriend, San Anselmo Prep's golden boy*: When Avery said she wanted to talk to me, I braced for impact. But she was incredibly polite when she stopped me by my

251

locker and asked why I'd broken up with her. You know who wasn't polite? Hutch, of all people. He was standing behind her with his arms crossed, glaring at me like I'd just broken his beakers. I have no idea why. Hutch and I have always gotten along pretty well.

HUTCH: No, no, I don't have a problem with Luke Murphy. I don't know why you would say that. I have been perfectly polite during every interaction I've ever had with him.

Editor's Note: Hutch honestly looked like he was going to murder Luke. Probably because he couldn't fly over to Italy and murder Fabrizio.

LUKE: Listen—I know the timing was bad, and I'm sorry. Avery was a good girlfriend—no, a *great* girlfriend. She's smart, funny, fun to be with, all that stuff. But it didn't really seem like she was that into me. Honestly? I kind of felt like there was maybe someone else she was into. And I didn't really want to go to prom with someone who just wasn't feeling it.

TRIPP GOMEZ-PARKER: Luke's a freak, man. Don't get me wrong. I love that kid, but who spends this much mental energy on feelings? Who *cares* who's feeling what or not feeling what? I'll never understand why he dumped Avery. At least now he was free to snap up all the saddos who couldn't get dates to prom, but I knew he wouldn't do that—because he's Luke Murphy. This whole thing was a Catch-32, man.

LUKE: Who was Avery into? No idea. I just knew she wasn't into me.

Editor's Note: Well, at least I feel less dumb for not realizing that I liked Hutch sooner. Apparently, nobody knew!

COCO: Avery had grown so much. Not only over our lifetime of friendship, but over the past couple weeks, too. She didn't yell at Luke or anything! And it struck me that Avery had broken up with all her boyfriends for the exact same reason Luke broke up with her. She just wasn't feeling it. They were just looking for the right person, and they weren't each other's right person. Do I think Hutch is Avery's right person? Maybe. They might seem really different on the surface . . . but the more I think about it, the more I think there's something about them that just fits.

HUTCH: We'd done it. AD had interviewed all of her ex-boyfriends. This was probably the largest mountain of data I'd sifted through in my career as a scientist.

AVERY: Had I learned more about myself? Absolutely. I couldn't stop thinking about what Coach Kelly said, about how tennis is different every time because you and your opponent are constantly changing. Some of my relationships had been great. Some of them had been pretty much the worst. But did I regret any of them? Not for a minute. They'd all changed me and made me who I am today. I'd learned something from each one of my ex-boyfriends, and I was pretty sure they'd learned something from me, too.

HUTCH: I thought back to *Roman Holiday*, and Avery's idea that you can be in love with an experience. Each one of her relationships had been an experience, and although she'd never been in love with any of those guys, I think she'd been in love with those experiences. And that was the important thing—it was those experiences that made Avery who she is. She wasn't defined by her past relationships, but she'd learned something from each one, and that made them important.

AVERY: I was still thinking about why all my relationships had ended. It would have been easy to say, "All my relationships ended because none of them had been with Hutch!" But although that was flattering to Hutch, I knew he would never accept such a simplistic conclusion. And besides, we'd only been dating for like forty-eight hours. That seemed a little presumptuous.

HUTCH: I remember the first experiments I'd done, back in elementary school, where everything had a clear-cut answer. You make a tornado in a bottle. You make rock candy. Boom. Done. But in real science, as in real life, there are no easy answers. AD's relationships had ended because she just wasn't that into them. Because she was searching for a better boyfriend. Because no one could date someone whose mom cuts his meat for him. There was no one answer, because her relationships had been as complex and varied as AD herself. In the end, though, I don't think it necessarily mattered *why* her relationships ended. What mattered was that AD knew that all of these relationships had been worthwhile—that she'd learned something from them, or they'd changed her in some way. More importantly, I think AD had learned that she didn't *need* a boyfriend—but she just might want one. How's that for a conclusion, AD? Now if you'll excuse me, I need to find a tux.

Editor's Note: Don't worry, Ms. Segerson—I'm sure you're dying to hear about prom, too! I wouldn't leave you hanging. I can't believe you didn't chaperone this year! I'll try to get over your betrayal, but it'll be tough. Did Emma Rajpur actually show up? Did Coco escape Tripp Gomez-Parker's clutches? Did I convince Hutch to actually dance and not just sit in the corner? Read on to find out!

THE PROM

LIAM PADALECKI: I showed up at Michael's house *stoked* for Ultimate Game Night. I know Michael's mom had been to Costco and gotten a ton of stuff, but I also arrived armed with three party-size bags of Cheetos Flamin' Hot Puffs, because I have very specific snack preferences.

Editor's Note: Don't worry, I power-washed his mouth with Listerine before Emma Rajpur showed up.

ALEX MANEVITZ: Of course I wasn't happy that Ultimate Game Night was being postponed! The entire point of Ultimate Game Night was that we weren't going to prom, and now, here we were: going to prom!

MICHAEL FEELEY: Alex was complaining nonstop about going to the prom, but I knew, deep down, somewhere in his tiny heart, he was happy that Liam got to meet Emma Rajpur. Besides, Coco and Avery showed up at our house with four tuxes and free prom tickets, so it's not like he had anything to complain about.

Editor's Note: Okay, so this actually was a misappropriation of prom funds. Don't rat me out, Ms. Segerson! Bizzy Stanhope never has to know!

COCO: I know Michael, Alex, Liam, and Hutch aren't exactly thought of as the studliest guys in our grade, but if you simply consider the base materials, free from any social prejudices, none of them are actually bad-looking. I was able to accomplish wonders with a hairbrush and some texturizing paste. And Michael even let Avery do his eyebrows! It was a vast improvement.

Editor's Note: Don't worry, I didn't let Coco go near any of them with scissors.

LIAM: It was kind of weird when Coco and Avery showed up with prom tickets and tuxes, but I guess it made sense. Now that Hutch and Avery were together, or whatever it means when you kiss someone on pretty much the last day of school, it seemed only natural that she would want Hutch and the rest of our social group to go to prom.

HUTCH: It was kind of amazing, the way she talked all of the guys into going to prom. By the end of the conversation, I think they were convinced that it was *their* idea, and that they'd wanted to go to prom all along. This is exactly why AD would be an extremely effective but terrifying politician. I can't believe I'm about to say this out loud, but I think Principal Patel did the right thing when he instituted that Student Council term limit.

Editor's Note: BETRAYAL! BETRAYAL OF THE HIGHEST ORDER! HOW DARE YOU, HUTCH?!

MICHAEL: Did I ever think I would see a day when Coco Kim and Avery Dennis were in my house? In my *bedroom*?! No, no, I did not. I suppose it was like in medieval times, when the Lord of Misrule upended the social order for the English elite during Yuletide. Avery Dennis was like the Lady of Misrule for the prom.

ALEX: They stormed in like they were on some kind of nerd makeover show. It was insulting! I can't believe Michael let Avery Dennis pluck his eyebrows. I lost whatever modicum of respect I had for him.

Editor's Note: Joke's on Alex, because Michael looked hot.

LIAM: Hutch told me he and Avery kissed like sixty seconds after it happened. Was I surprised? No. Hutch has been pretty much obsessed with Avery for as long as I've known him. "Blah blah blah, Avery writes the best lab reports, blah blah blah, Avery can dissect a frog better than you, blah blah blah, Avery can find so many protozoa when she looks through a microscope," and on and on and on. He never came right out and said, "I am secretly and desperately in love with my lab partner," but it was obvious to anyone with ears. Well, if anything, I was *maybe* surprised that Avery turned out to be secretly obsessed with Hutch, too, but I guess no one is that thorough in their lab reports unless they have a really good reason. I think Hutch was worried that I was going to be weird about it, given my dating history, but I am totally cool. Seventh grade was practically the Mesozoic Era. The wounds had healed. As long as Hutch always remembered that *I* dated Avery *first*, he could date her as long as he wanted. I hoped one day I could give the best-man speech at their wedding, so my very last line could be "And let's never forget—*I* dated her *first*. Cheers to the bride and groom!"

Editor's Note: Wedding?! Liam was getting a leeettle ahead of himself.

COCO: We were so busy getting the boys ready, *we* almost forgot to get ready, too! I had never imagined that I'd spend senior prom getting ready at Michael Feeley's house, but I was getting ready with Avery, and that's all that really mattered.

AVERY: Coco can get kind of mushy at important lifetime events.

COCO: I'd known Avery since we were babies, and now here we were, getting ready for prom together! I'm sorry, just . . . give me a minute.

Editor's Note: What a mush. She had to dig her Wonder Woman Kleenex out of her purse.

ALEX: Coco and Avery kicked us all out of Michael's room so they could get ready. Of course, Mrs. Feeley forced us into a horrible photo shoot. It was mortifying. If Mrs. Feeley hadn't put out that spread of pigs in a blanket, the entire night would have been a complete waste.

HUTCH: When AD walked down the stairs, I didn't . . . I couldn't . . . There were no words. You know what's crazy? Prom literally *just* happened. And I can't remember her dress. Not at all. Not the color, the style, nothing. All I can remember is how beautiful she looked, how her whole face just *glowed,* and I couldn't believe that someone so incredible wanted to spend her prom with me.

Editor's Note: It was strapless, black and white, and as similar to Audrey Hepburn's dress in Sabrina *as was physically possible. But more importantly, Hutch looked so incredibly handsome in his tux I almost didn't recognize him. I mean, not that he's not* always *handsome, he's just not always . . . well . . . He looked good in the tux. Let's just leave it at that.*

MICHAEL: Avery looked very pretty, but Coco in that slinky silver dress . . . She looked like a Bond girl! I wished I'd given stupid Tripp Gomez-Parker the wrong directions to my house so I would have *had* to take her instead.

Editor's Note: That actually would have been completely adorable! Also, I kind of can't believe Coco's mom let her get that dress. On a scale of one to Bizzy Stanhope, it was definitely conservative, but pretty risqué for Coco! She obviously completely rocked it.

TRIPP GOMEZ-PARKER: Yeah, I thought it was weird that I was picking Coco up for the prom at Michael Feeley's house. Michael Feeley? Seriously?! Didn't ask, though. Assumed it was some weird Avery thing, and decided I'd rather not know.

I'd borrowed my cousin's sweet red Mustang convertible to pick her up in. I knew all those nerds' eyes were gonna pop out of their heads when I picked her up.

COCO: Tripp is lucky I decided to blow my hair out and wear it straight. Otherwise I would have *murdered* him for driving a convertible to prom. As it is, I look a little more windswept in our prom photos than I would have preferred.

TRIPP: And then when I finally got to Feeley's house, Coco wouldn't let me leave! I was trapped there! As I pulled up, I honked, but she didn't come out, so I honked again. Still no Coco! After four or five honks, I gave up and went to the door.

COCO: Oh, as *if* I was going to run to the door when Tripp honked! Like I was a . . . a . . . delivery pizza or something! No. If he wanted me to get in the car, he could come to the door like a gentleman.

TRIPP: Feeley let me in, and he looked like he wanted to murder me, for whatever reason. Grumpy little dude. There was something different about his face, too, but I couldn't quite put my finger on it. It was freaking me out, man! It was so lame to be trapped in a room with those weirdos, but at least there were pigs in a blanket. And Coco looked hot, as I knew she would.

Editor's Note: No one is overselling Mrs. Feeley's pigs in a blanket. They were beyond delicious.

COCO: Of course I wasn't going to leave before Emma Rajpur got there! Are you kidding?! I was dying to see the big moment!

LIAM: Avery was acting nuts. She said she'd booked a limo and it hadn't come yet. She was pacing around the room, looking through the blinds every minute, and growling things like "Come on, come on, where are you?!"

AVERY: I was panicking. Where was she?! Emma Rajpur was five minutes late, and I was convinced she'd decided not to come at all. Maybe bottled water was back on-brand again! Who knows with these flaky Hollywood types!

LIAM: The limo pulled up, and Avery shot out of the door.

AVERY: I had to get the perfect angle! I wanted to capture the whole thing on my cell phone so I could record it for posterity. And maybe remix it and make Liam Padalecki a YouTube star.

TRIPP: Coco bounced out of the house. I stuffed a couple of pigs in a blanket in my pockets and followed her.
Editor's Note: Later on in the evening, all of the pigs in a blanket were smushed in the wake of a particularly enthusiastic worm. Tripp ate them anyway.

HUTCH: The entire motley crew was assembled on the front lawn to watch Emma Rajpur's limo pull into the driveway. Me,

Avery, Michael, Liam, Alex, Coco, Tripp Gomez-Parker, and Michael's mom. It was a group I would have previously thought could only come together in a very strange dream.

LIAM: I had no idea why everyone was freaking out. I think we'd all seen limos before.

AVERY: I watched through the screen on my phone as the limo pulled up. The driver got out and opened the door. One long, tan leg emerged, followed by the rest of Emma Rajpur in a slit-to-there black dress. Couldn't wait to see her try to get that one past Principal Patel.

LIAM: It didn't even hit me who it was at first. I just saw a hot girl coming out of a limo. But then she got closer, and it was Emma Rajpur. *Emma Rajpur!* She looked just like she did in my poster, and on TV every week, only even more perfect, somehow. She was also tinier than I'd ever imagined—only as tall as my shoulder.

COCO: She was completely poreless. Seriously. There was not a flaw on her face. She looked like she'd been airbrushed!

HUTCH: Liam was completely awestruck. I pushed him, and he staggered toward Emma Rajpur.

COCO: She was so smiley. Insanely white teeth. I think I was staring at her in a weird way, but honestly, she was *blinding*.

263

Tripp maneuvered me into his car, and then Hutch got Liam and everybody into the limo.

MICHAEL: Alex immediately started quizzing poor Emma Rajpur on scientific impossibilities in the *Skyward* universe. I had to save her—and Liam. So I went to my go-to Alex distracting conversation topic, which is "Jurassic Park could easily happen within the next five years."

ALEX: Jurassic Park is not happening anytime soon. It's not! It is absolutely not!

HUTCH: There was a lot of background noise about Jurassic Park, but even though there were six people in that limo, all I could see was Avery. I realize she was sitting next to someone who was professionally beautiful, but Emma Rajpur couldn't hold a candle to Avery. I reached out and grabbed her hand. She leaned her head against my shoulder, and I think that was the moment I changed my mind about prom. Prom was awesome. We could have just ridden around the block in the limo, and I would have been happy.

AVERY: We pulled up at the planetarium, and everyone looked amazingly nice, even the teachers who were chaperoning. I realize that everyone was staring at and taking pictures of Emma Rajpur, not me, but I still felt like a celebrity, too.

COCO: I don't think it was even Emma Rajpur. Everyone was staring at Michael Feeley's eyebrows. His face had been transformed!

Editor's Note: I love that Coco has so much faith in my aesthetician prowess, but I am really confident that everyone was staring at Emma Rajpur, not Michael Feeley's eyebrows.

AVERY: As we walked toward the planetarium, I squeezed Hutch's hand. I was so nervous—I hoped everyone in our class liked the way the room looked. It was a lot of pressure, being head of the Prom Committee! But then the doors opened, and the space was even more magical than I remembered. It was midnight in Paris at six forty-five in San Francisco.

HUTCH: You know what? It really didn't look half-bad. Pretty impressive for a bunch of tech kids with glue guns.

COCO: How did Avery pull it off?! I mean seriously, how?! I had seen those balloons with my very own eyes. I was there when Bizzy announced there was no longer a venue. There was nothing left in the budget. Where did all this come from? How did she even get into this space?!

BIZZY STANHOPE: I have no idea how she pulled it off.

COCO: All Avery would say is "Hutch did it," and then smile. That wasn't a real answer!

BIZZY STANHOPE: Tamsin's, um, unfortunate mistake had guaranteed there would be no decorations. And Daddy's scheduling conflict had guaranteed there would be no venue. And yet, here it was! A venue! Decorated! It was totally tacky, but it was still more than I expected. Whatever. Prom's stupid anyway. Like who cares, right? I can't wait until I get to college and I can plan formals at my sorority and they can be *real* events, not like this amateurish hoedown Avery had planned.

Editor's Note: Dear God, please protect the future sorority sisters of Bizzy Stanhope.

TAMSIN BREWER: It was so pretty in there! Bizzy was mad about something, but I'm not sure what. She was so grumpy!

Editor's Note: Tamsin Brewer's date was the Minion balloon. She did let Coco take a picture with it at least.

CRESSIDA SCHROBENHAUSER-CLONAN: When I walked into the prom, the first thing I saw was Avery Dennis holding hands with Hutch. Of course she was. Because Avery Dennis gets absolutely everything she wants. Now there was absolutely no reason for me to be there, except that my mom made me come. God, I hope college is better than high school.

LIAM: Prom was one of the best nights of my life. Did Emma Rajpur and I fall in love? No. But it turns out, she is *awesome*. She's kind of a goofy dancer, so she made me feel better about my goofy dancing. And she loves the *Skyward* universe just as much as I do! She's also really into graphic novels, and vegan baking, and hiking with her dog. I thought she might just stay for a PR photo op and leave, but she stayed for the whole prom. And she gave me her secret Facebook account name so we could stay in touch. Promises were made about *Skyward* season four spoilers . . . and I'm going to hold her to that.

MICHAEL: Prom was the best night of my life.

COCO: I think I broke the prom date Code of Ethics.

MICHAEL: I guess Avery was right, when she was going on and on and on about how prom is a magical night where anything can happen. Because I sure felt the magic.

COCO: Listen, I know I am not, was not, and will never be Tripp Gomez-Parker's girlfriend, but I do feel like there is an implied pledge of fidelity when you agree to go to the prom with someone. But I couldn't help myself! I blame it on the eyebrows.

MICHAEL: Coco Kim is probably the most beautiful person I've ever seen in real life. But I thought a universe in which someone like me could kiss someone like Coco was purely theoretical.

COCO: I ran into Michael on my way back from the bathroom, and we were alone in a darkened hallway.

MICHAEL: She pulled me toward her like she was Neodymium Iron Boron and I was a metal filing. I was powerless to resist.

COCO: I kissed him, okay?! It was me! It was all me! I abandoned my date and made out with Michael Feeley in the hallway for an inappropriately long time!

TRIPP: Yeah, Coco disappeared for a weirdly long time, but it was fine. I danced with Tamsin Brewer. She still looked banging, even with that weird yellow balloon tied around her wrist.

COCO: Good God . . . maybe *I'm* JFK! JFK probably made out with tons of randos at White House dinners!

MICHAEL: Best. Night. Ever.

HUTCH: We stayed until the very last song of the night and the teachers kicked us out. Avery and I danced to almost every song. We went back to the ice-cream sundae bar three times. And we kissed in a surprisingly unsupervised hallway. I hadn't had that much fun since the Intel International Science and Engineering Fair.

Editor's Note: Coming from Hutch, this is a MAJOR compliment. Also, what did I tell you about that hallway, Ms. Segerson?! I bet you'll chaperone next year!

AVERY: Somehow . . . Bizzy Stanhope and Sean Graney were voted Prom Queen and King. Did I suspect that she'd cheated, somehow, and rigged the voting? Sure. But you know what? I couldn't have cared less. Let Bizzy have her shiny piece of plastic if it meant that much to her. Because prom was over after a few magical hours, but then we were cruising through the In-N-Out drive-through in a limo, and I had successfully kidnapped Coco from Tripp Gomez-Parker—at the time, I didn't realize that Michael Feeley also had something to do with it, but who could have seen that coming?! There I was, sitting with my best friend and my, well, my Hutch, eating animal fries and drinking a strawberry vanilla milk shake and laughing like I couldn't ever remember laughing before. And *that's* what prom is really about. One last perfect moment with the people you love in high school. It might have been the happiest moment of my life—so far.

HUTCH: Avery wouldn't stop harassing me about the onions on my burger. I'll convert her one of these days, though.

MICHAEL: My mom called Coco and Avery's parents and got their permission for them to sleep over at my place, since my mom assured them Coco and Avery could share the guest room, she would personally be supervising at all times, and there would be absolutely no funny business, blah blah blah. Miracles really *do* happen on prom night! Because Coco Kim and Avery Dennis were sleeping at my house, and they said they wanted to play D&D with us.

ALEX: They completely destroyed our rate of play. Not to mention that they don't have the group camaraderie the four of us had established over the past four years. Or the fact that they decided to be twin elven archers named Mary-Kate and Ashley Olsen.

LIAM: Alex is just mad that Avery had a higher kill rate than he did.

ALEX: Listen—I think we all saw firsthand exactly what happens when you date the Dungeon Master.

HUTCH: I cannot *believe* he said that! No one has ever—*ever*—cast aspersions on my integrity as a Dungeon Master. And I swear to you on the hammer of Thor that I didn't do *anything* in AD's favor. That was a totally straight game. She was just that good. Beginner's luck, maybe, but she was good. Sour grapes, man.

MICHAEL: Avery was actually pretty decent. With more playing, I think she could be great. Coco . . . not so much. Although she kissed me when she got her one and only hit of the campaign, and *that* was great.

Editor's Note: I was so surprised when Coco kissed Michael Feeley, one of Liam's Flamin' Hot Cheetos fell out of my mouth. Just fell right out of my mouth and onto the board. Alex Manevitz sighed really loudly and brushed my Cheeto dust away with way more force than was necessary.

COCO: Would I play again? Probably not—I am legitimately *awful* at D&D. But I never thought I'd have so much fun being awful at something! Or that I would spend the rest of my prom night in Michael Feeley's dining room playing a tabletop RPG game instead of at the after-party at Tripp Gomez-Parker's house.

TRIPP: Oh, yeah . . . I guess Coco never did make it to my house. I hooked up with Tamsin Brewer, though, so it's all good. It was kind of weird, though, because she wouldn't put down that yellow Minion balloon.
Editor's Note: SO MANY bullets dodged on prom night!

MICHAEL: My mom never did have to worry about those guest rooms.

LIAM: Just like we'd all hoped, on Ultimate Game Night, we raged till dawn.

MICHAEL: As the sun rose, I popped a bunch of Eggo waffles into the toaster. The way Coco ate her waffle was so cute . . . She nibbled it like a little squirrel.
Editor's Note: Coco does look like a squirrel when she eats with her hands! We used to call ourselves Squirrel Girl and Piranha Woman. (I've been told I look a little toothy while I eat.)

HUTCH: I could tell AD was getting tired. Her head kept nodding onto my shoulder, and every once in a while, she'd jerk herself up with a start and shout, "Kill the kobolds!"

Editor's Note: "Aggressive, xenophobic, yet industrious small humanoid creatures, kobolds are noted for their skill at building traps and preparing ambushes."—Wikipedia

AVERY: I didn't want to miss a minute, but I must have fallen asleep at some point, because Hutch shook me and whispered, "AD," until I woke up with the box top from the Eggo waffles stuck to my face.

HUTCH: Ultimate Game Night was over. Prom was over, too. I was sad, but man, it had been fun while it lasted.

AVERY: Hutch and Michael walked me and Coco to the car. I had a lot of questions about *that* situation I was planning to ask once we got in the car, but at that moment, Hutch was kissing me, and I had absolutely no brain space for Michael Feeley.

HUTCH: I kissed AD good-bye. I didn't know where, or even if, I'd ever see her again.

THE END

(Just kidding, Ms. Segerson! I wouldn't leave you hanging like that!)

JAMES "HUTCH" HUTCHERSON

HUTCH: I first saw Avery Dennis in a pink bikini at a pool party. I met her on the first day of freshman biology. And I was mildly annoyed when she turned to me and asked for a pencil because she'd forgotten hers. Which she would proceed to do, every single day, for the next four years. But I quickly learned that AD's inability to hold on to a pencil—despite having more colored pens than any human reasonably should—was only a very small part of who she is. I probably started to fall in love with her the first day I saw her dissect a frog. Or maybe it was the day she wrote that song about enzyme catalysis and sang it in her horrible, wonderful, off-key voice. Maybe it was all of those days, and more. And she must have been falling in love with me, too, or she *never* would have broken her oath to stop dating.

AVERY: I met James "Hutch" Hutcherson on the first day of freshman biology when I asked him for a pencil. I spent the next four years looking forward to science class every single day, but somehow didn't realize that was because of Hutch until the last week of school.

HUTCH: My friends have been asking me a lot about what happens next with me and AD. I know there's this stereotype that guys don't like to talk about relationships, but Michael and Liam have been bugging me nonstop about what our "label" is.

AVERY: How would I label us? I don't know. Happy? I'm just happy I realized I liked Hutch before it was too late. Also, I'm happy that Coco found Ashley Jenkins on Facebook, and was able to confirm through mutual friends that she'd never dated Hutch. Not that it really matters, since I am the last person who has any right to be jealous about exes, but at least we solved that mystery. Although I should have known from the start that Hutch would *never* date someone who would incorrectly label a diagram. The mantle is like the easiest layer of the Earth to identify.

HUTCH: Michael kept wailing that we'd found each other "too late." But I don't think that's true at all. Caltech and Pepperdine are only an hour apart, after all.

AVERY: So we're seeing what happens. We're taking it slow. And we're still together. Although I don't know how I'm going to get pencils in college.

HUTCH: I wasn't sure I wanted to be in Avery's oral history project. I don't want to be her past. I want to be her present. And, hopefully, her future.

AVERY: But that's the thing about history, right, Ms. Segerson? It's still being written, all the time, even while we're living it.

Now it was time for me to close the book on my history of boys, open up my yearbook, collect signatures from absolutely *everyone*, and get ready to graduate. As I flipped through the pages that contained our final legacy as seniors at San Anselmo Prep, I had another epiphany about history. History may help us understand *why* certain events had happened. But maybe the most important thing wasn't the why, but that we remember. That we have a record of the experiences that we loved and the people we loved having them with. Because I was happy that I had a better understanding of *why* my relationships had ended, but I was even happier that along the way, I'd made so many wonderful friends, had so many amazing experiences, and had so many ways to remember them by. So I guess you were right, Ms. Segerson. History is pretty worthwhile after all. But I think I'm done with writing history for a while. It's time for me to *make* history instead.

> *Avery:*
> *This was extremely unorthodox, and yet I must say I'm impressed by how thorough you were.*
>
> # A+
>
> *Good luck at Pepperdine—don't be a stranger.*
>
> *—Ms. Segerson*

ACKNOWLEDGMENTS

This book is the fulfillment of my lifelong dream to write a book for Scholastic. If elementary school me, whose favorite day of the year was the Scholastic Book Fair, could see me now, she would probably pee her pants. Huge thank-yous are in order to everyone who made this dream come true.

Matt Ringler, thank you for coming up with this brilliant concept and for entrusting it to me. Writing an oral history has been frequently fun, sometimes frustrating, but always fascinating. This book would literally not exist without you, and it wouldn't be nearly as good without your pitch-perfect editing and Kanye lyrics. I'm also convinced that if someone made an '80s-style workplace sitcom starring the two of us, it would be hilarious. Thank you to Jennifer Abbots, Michelle Campbell, Laura Festa, and everyone at Scholastic I haven't had the pleasure of e-meeting yet. Your love for this book overwhelms me, in the best possible way.

Molly Ker Hawn, you are a dream-come-true agent and one of my favorite people. Thank you, thank you, thank you for sending this project my way. Thank you for being my best early reader, and for always making me feel like I'm funny. I should probably just move to London so we can have brunch all the time, right?

Max, by the time you read this, we'll be married! Thank you for reading every page and for always having faith in my writing, even when I don't. I wish I was half the genius you think I am, but I love you for thinking it. Additional thanks to you, Daniel and Colin for keeping my D&D references honest and for introducing me to the wonderful world of tabletop gaming. I will beat all of you at Lords of Waterdeep anytime, anyplace. Especially you, Colin. I will destroy you.

Dad, thanks for all those emails saying "good" to let me know I'm on the right track. Mom, thank you for your constant love and support, and for always picking up the phone, even if it's the fourth time I've called that day. Ali, remember that time your hair was doing a thing? Yeah, me too. Thanks for that. Somers and Max (again!), thanks for the conversation about helicopter parents that spawned a great chapter.

I thought I hated high school when I was there, but now I realize how great it was, if only because I had incredible teachers and made amazing friends. Mr. Burns and Ms. Schwartz, you are the kind of English teachers people write inspirational movies about; Mr. Campbell and Mr. Guffin, I know you would *never* have given this history project an A+, but all four of you made me a writer. Megan, Donnie, Sarah, Evie, and Caitlin—I'd still share a prom limo with all of you. Let me know when the DJ plays "Hey Ya!," okay?

ABOUT THE AUTHOR

Author photo by Braden Nesin

Stephanie Kate Strohm is the author of *Pilgrims Don't Wear Pink*, *Confederates Don't Wear Couture*, and *The Taming of the Drew*. She graduated from Middlebury College with a dual degree in theater and history and has acted her way around the United States, performing in more than twenty-five states. She currently lives in Chicago with her fiancé and a dog named Lorelei Lee.